Praise for

I0658959

Poker Night

Texas Hold 'em is a well-written story that flows well
from the first meeting till the end. The love scenes are
scorchers and WOW they are sexy and hot. Carol
Lynne knows how to bring her characters to living
life. This one will stay in my keeper file.
~*Night Owl Romance*

I love Carol Lynne and her talent for creating
wonderful characters that immediately grab your
heart and refuse to let go...if you are looking for a
smoking hot read with great characters this is the
story for you! ~ *Fallen Angels Reviews*

Slow-Play is book two in the Poker Night series and
just as good as the first...I can't wait to read book
three of this series! ~ *Fallen Angels Reviews*

Carol Lynne proves that literary gay sex does not
have to be rough to be exciting, and that love is a
universal turn-on ~ *Author, Lisabet Sarai*

Total-E-Bound Publishing books in print from
Carol Lynne:

Campus Cravings Volume One: On the Field
Coach
Side-Lined
Sacking the Quarterback

Campus Cravings Volume Two: Off the Field
Off Season
Forbidden Freshman

Campus Cravings Volume Three: Back on Campus
Broken Pottery
In Bear's Bed

Campus Cravings Volume Four: Dorm Life
Office Advances
A Biker's Vow

Campus Cravings Volume Five: BK House
Hershie's Kiss
Theron's Return

Good-Time Boys
Sonny's Salvation
Garron's Gift
Rawley's Redemption
Twin Temptations

Cattle Valley Volume One
All Play & No Work
Cattle Valley Mistletoe

Cattle Valley Volume Two
Sweet Topping
Rough Ride

Cattle Valley Volume Three
Physical Therapy
Out of the Shadow

Cattle Valley Volume Four
Bad Boy Cowboy
The Sound of White

Cattle Valley Volume Five
Gone Surfin'
The Last Bouquet

POKER NIGHT
Volume One

Texas Hold 'em

Slow-Play

CAROL LYNNE

Poker Night: Volume One
ISBN # 978-1-907010-92-7
©Copyright Carol Lynne 2009
Cover Art by April Martinez ©Copyright 2009
Interior text design by Claire Siemaszkiewicz
Total-E-Bound Publishing

This is a work of fiction. All characters, places and events are from the author's imagination and should not be confused with fact. Any resemblance to persons, living or dead, events or places is purely coincidental.

All rights reserved. No part of this publication may be reproduced in any material form, whether by printing, photocopying, scanning or otherwise without the written permission of the publisher, Total-E-Bound Publishing.

Applications should be addressed in the first instance, in writing, to Total-E-Bound Publishing. Unauthorised or restricted acts in relation to this publication may result in civil proceedings and/or criminal prosecution.

The author and illustrator have asserted their respective rights under the Copyright Designs and Patents Acts 1988 (as amended) to be identified as the author of this book and illustrator of the artwork. Published in 2009 by Total-E-Bound Publishing Faldingworth Road, Spridlington, Market Rasen, Lincolnshire, LN8 2DE, UK.

No part of this book may be reproduced, scanned, or distributed in any printed or electronic form without permission. Please do not participate in or encourage piracy of copyrighted materials in violation of the authors' rights. Purchase only authorised copies. Total-E-Bound Publishing is an imprint of Total-E-Ntwined Limited.

If you purchased this book without a cover you should be aware that this book is stolen property. It was reported as "unsold and destroyed" to the publisher and neither the author nor the publisher has received any payment for this "stripped book".
Manufactured in the USA.

TEXAS
HOLD 'EM

Dedication

For Michael Chamberlain and Angelo Cicatello.
Here are your books about average men doing
average jobs, well mostly.

Chapter One

Zac parked in front of his second-storey garage apartment and turned off the ignition. He hated running late, even when it wasn't his fault. He jumped out of his four-year-old Jeep Wrangler and grabbed the gym bag beside him.

He wasn't surprised to find his friend Marco sitting on the top step. "Sorry," Zac said, stepping around Marco to unlock the door. "The team bus had a flat on the way home from Santa Cruz."

"No problem," Marco returned, standing. "Kent has me working way up north. I hoped you'd take pity on me and let me shower the stink off here instead of going all the way home."

Zac glanced over his shoulder at the filthy brick layer, and stepped inside his apartment. "As long as you promise to scrub the tub out when you're done. Last time I let you take a shower, I could've grown potatoes in there afterward."

Marco snorted. "Okey dokey, country boy." Marco started to walk towards the bathroom, but stopped. "Hey, uh, don't suppose I could borrow a pair of shorts or sweats or something?"

Zac rolled his eyes and tossed his keys on the table. A quick glance at the clock told him the rest of the guys would be there any minute. "Bottom drawer, but cinch up tight this time, will ya? I'd rather not spend all evening looking at the top of your bush."

Marco chuckled. "You love my sexy bush, and you know it." Marco gave Zac an air kiss and strolled away.

After cleaning up his breakfast dishes and wiping down the counter, Zac retreated to his bedroom. A quick change into a pair of faded red sweats and a Forty-Niners T-shirt and he was ready for poker night.

He heard the front door open and shut and knew it had to be Bobby. His oldest friend in the bay area, Bobby Quinn always made himself at home, no matter where he was. "Hey," Zac greeted as he walked into the kitchen.

Bobby already had his head stuck in the fridge. "Got anything to eat? The charter ran long and the snobs I took out didn't even offer their leftovers."

"Cookies, top shelf." Zac opened the storage closet and pulled out two of the extra dining chairs. "Should I put the leaf in the table? Seemed kinda crowded last time."

Bobby tried to answer around a mouthful of chocolate wafer cookies, spraying crumbs all over Zac's clean kitchen floor. Bobby grinned and swallowed. "Sorry, dude. Yeah. I'd like a little more elbow room."

Zac pointed towards the crumbs. "Clean those up, you pig." He opened the storage door once more and lifted out the heavy oak table leaf. He hadn't purchased much when he moved to California from Idaho, but as soon as he started the bi-weekly poker night with his friends, he'd gone out and bought a dining room set big enough to accommodate the six of them. Of course the set didn't match anything else he had, and it was too big for the small apartment, but he made it work. "Hey, see if I have any chips in the cupboard."

With the leaf in place, Zac arranged the chairs accordingly. He loved poker night. Hell, he loved his friends, even if some of them were a slovenly bunch.

"Half a bag of barbecue and some green onion," Bobby said, turning his nose up.

"Shit." Zac picked up the phone and called Kent.

"Baker," Kent answered.

"Hey, can you do me a big one and stop and get a couple bags of chips, maybe a bag of pretzels?" Zac asked.

"Sure. I was gonna stop and pick up some more beer anyway. Trey never brings enough, and Angelo only brings that flavoured pussy beer."

Zac chuckled. "I'd have never put Angelo and the word pussy in the same sentence. Besides, it's just Mexican beer. He puts the lime in it, it doesn't come that way."

"Whatever," Kent drawled. "I'll be there in twenty, as long as the traffic gods are smiling on me."

Zac hung up the phone and turned back to Bobby. "I guess I'm not a very good host this week. I'll call and order some pizza later."

Bobby finished off the cookies in his hand and opened a bottle of water. "Serves them right. They should be bringing stuff. It's not fair for you to always fork over the cash to feed us."

Zac leaned his hip against the table and crossed his arms. "Yeah? And what did you bring?" He softened the question with a wry grin.

"My sparkling personality, and this smokin' hot bod," Bobby answered. "What more could a night with a bunch of queers need?"

"A nine-inch dick?"

Bobby grabbed his basket and snorted. "Got one of those right here."

Zac started laughing. "Yeah, sure."

Bobby started to unbutton his jeans. "Want me to prove it?"

Zac held up his hand. "No. I may not have had a date in a while, but I don't need you waving your willy around."

Bobby shrugged. "Your loss." He wandered out of the kitchen into the living room and flopped down on Zac's worn red couch.

"Turn on the news," Zac instructed, walking into the room. "They should have highlights from the game."

Bobby did so. "Sorry, forgot to ask. You guys win?"

"Of course," Zac said, puffing just a tad. His team was undefeated, and Zac had high hopes of making it all the way to the state championship.

The door opened and Trey walked in, carrying a case of beer. "Could I get a little help?"

Zac stood and easily lifted the beer out of his friend's hands. Trey was a fantastic guy but strong he wasn't. With a law degree in his hip pocket, Trey had decided to go against his family and become a teacher, much to his father's disapproval.

Zac took the beer into the kitchen and set it on the counter. Getting into the freezer, he pulled out the bag of ice he'd remembered to buy a couple of days earlier and carried it to the sink. After filling the sink with ice and bottles, he returned to the living room carrying four beers. He passed them out, eyeing Marco as he handed one over. "You clean the tub?"

"Yes, Mom," Marco answered. "I even hung up the towel."

Zac nodded and took a seat on the couch between Bobby and Trey. As the weatherman gave the work-week forecast, Zac took a long pull from his beer. "Heard from my sister Beth the other day," he offered to no one in particular. "She's having twins."

Bobby clapped him on the back. "Congrats, Uncle Zac."

Zac grinned. He already had four nieces and three nephews, but he couldn't wait for the new babies to arrive. There was just something about the smell of a baby Zac couldn't get enough of. It reminded him he needed to make arrangements to fly back home to Houston for Thanksgiving. He just prayed the tickets weren't as high as they were at Easter.

A knock sounded at the door. Zac stood and looked at his buddies. "See? Some people have manners."

"Yeah. You know it has to be Angelo," Marco scoffed. "Betcha he's wearing a suit, too."

Chuckling, Zac opened the door to...yep, Angelo. Marco had been wrong, though. Angelo wasn't wearing a suit this time. Zac's guess was the ribbing he'd taken two weeks prior had been enough to persuade him into wearing jeans and a starched button down shirt instead. A sales manager for the top rated radio station in the bay area, Angelo always seemed to be in business mode.

"Hey," Angelo greeted, holding up two six packs of Corona beer, a bag of limes clutched in his fist.

"Put 'em in the sink," Zac told him, sitting back down on the couch. He glanced around the room at his friends. Who would've thought a group of guys from such different backgrounds and vocations would manage to find friendship in each other?

He'd met Bobby when he was down for a job interview at the local high school. Zac had decided to wander the marina to get a better feel for Pacifica, the town where he'd be coaching. He'd struck up a conversation with Bobby in one of the little bars near the beach and they'd been friends since.

Bobby had introduced Zac to Marco. Marco had introduced them both to his boss, Kent, and Kent had introduced them to Angelo. Zac met Trey on his first day on the job. He'd spotted Trey as a fellow gay man right away and had decided there was strength in numbers. That had been almost four years ago, and the group had played poker every other Saturday for a little more than three years.

"Stop staring at my feet, you perv," Marco growled at Angelo.

"I'm not. Get over yourself," Angelo countered, crossing his legs and appearing extremely uncomfortable.

Everyone in the room laughed. It was a well known fact Angelo Pilato had a strange foot fetish. According to Angelo, it wasn't a fetish. He simply found small feet on a man extremely attractive, especially if those feet happened to be encased in a pair of equally small athletic shoes.

A loud bang on the door signalled Kent's arrival. Since Kent was the last of their group to arrive, the gang headed into the kitchen. Kent handed the bag of munchies to Zac and carried the additional case of beer to the kitchen.

"Damn," Zac said. "We've got enough booze to get rip-roaring drunk."

"Yeah, well it's been that kinda week," Kent answered, twisting the cap off one of the already-chilled bottles.

Zac didn't miss the glance Kent made Marco's way as he said it. The two men had danced around each other's obvious attraction since he'd known them. Zac had even asked Kent about it early on in their friendship. Kent had simply replied that he wasn't a player and didn't much care for men who were.

It didn't take a rocket scientist to figure the situation out after that. Marco was indeed a player. Zac didn't know if Marco even bothered dating the same man twice. What neither of them could see was the fact they were both miserable. Zac wondered how Kent and Marco managed to maintain a friendship at all with the way they sniped at each other constantly.

Zac opened one of the bottom cupboards and pulled out the chips and cards. "Got a couple of brand new decks," he mentioned, tossing the cards on the table.

"Good," Kent commented, narrowing his eyes at Marco. "Maybe we can keep the corners from mysteriously getting bent on all the Aces."

"Fuck off," Marco countered.

Zac rolled his eyes. He could already tell it was going to be one of those nights. He'd be ready to strangle the two men by the time they were through their third hand. "I thought I'd order pizza. That sound okay?"

Everyone agreed but Angelo. "Thanks, but I had sushi on the way over."

"Of course you did," Bobby chuckled.

Kent shuffled the cards with skill before thumping the deck in front of Zac. "Your call."

Zac grinned, and passed the cards to Bobby to cut. "I'm from Houston, boys, it's gotta be Texas Hold 'em." Zac set the dealer button in front of him and dealt two cards, face down, to each player. Bobby, sitting immediately to his left put in his chip for the small blind, next to him, Kent added two chips to the pot for the big blind. The betting moved to Angelo who studied his cards and finally added two chips to the pile. After everyone had placed their bets, Zac dealt three cards in the centre of the table face up. These cards were known as 'The Flop'. Once again they went around the table, betting against their hands, Angelo was the first to fold.

"Okay, 'The Turn' card is...Ace of clubs," Zac announced.

When the betting resumed, Kent and Marco bowed out. Zac looked at his hole cards. He had a pair of Jacks, excellent cards. With the addition of the pair of sevens on the table, Zac tossed three more chips into the pot. "And 'The River' is...the Jack of hearts."

Zac schooled his face, refusing to let the glee he felt show in his expression. Bobby plunked down three more chips and Trey folded. Not interested in taking all of Bobby's money this early in the game, Zac merely called, putting in the required three chips. He turned over his cards with a grin. "Three Jacks," he crowed proudly.

Bobby tsked Zac when he started to reach for the pile of chips. "Three Aces," Bobby proclaimed, swatting Zac's hands away from his winnings.

"Fuck," Zac groaned. He stood and walked over to the phone. "I'm gonna call in the pizzas."

* * * *

Forty-five minutes and twenty-three bucks later, the doorbell rang. Zac stood and held out his hand to Bobby. "Come on, Mr. Big, fork over some pizza money."

Bobby chuckled, but gave Zac a twenty. "Hey, you're the guy from *Houston*. I can't help it if you suck at your own game."

With a sneer, Zac grabbed his wallet and went to answer the door. As soon as he opened it, his jaw dropped. There, standing on his porch was the sexiest man he'd laid eyes on since leaving college. "Damn," he whispered to himself.

The tiny little blond Adonis held up four square boxes. "Total comes to fifty-four-eleven."

Zac opened his wallet and pulled out two twenties, adding Bobby's twenty to the mix. "Keep the change." There was an awkward moment when the cute little blond went to pass the pizzas over. Zac felt the back of the guy's hand press against his half-hard cock, as he struggled to hand over the heavy stack of boxes. Trying to play it off, Zac joked. "I think feeling me up at least deserves an exchange of names. I'm Zac," he introduced himself.

"Huh?" The Adonis looked completely lost.

"My name's Zac. What's yours?"

"The guy eyed him suspiciously for a few seconds. Eric," he mumbled, turning around and retreating down the steps.

Zac leaned out the doorway and a pair of cute little buns as they slowly made their way back to the delivery car. "Mmm. Mmm. Mmm," Zac said, smacking his lips. "Maybe I need to order pizza more often."

He watched until the beat-up Toyota pulled out of the driveway before shutting the door. Zac carried the pizzas in and set them on the counter, catching a bit of the conversation in the process.

"I'm just saying, there's no reason why we couldn't have a martini night once in a while. Why does it always have to be beer," Angelo whined.

"Cuz we're men," Kent returned in apparent disgust.

Angelo shook his head and rolled his eyes. There was no doubt Angelo thought they were all a bunch of uncouth queers, but that's probably why Zac got along so well with them. He glanced around the apartment. Yeah, he didn't have a decorating bone in his body. There went the theory that shoving your cock up some guy's ass automatically made you a Martha Stewart clone.

The thought of fucking a tight little ass brought Eric to mind. Geez it had been a long dry spell, and never in his wildest dreams had he thought someone as gorgeous as that lived in the area. Where the hell had

Eric been keeping himself? Zac shook his head. He didn't know, but he damn well would be finding out if he had to gain ten pounds to do it.

Chapter Two

Eric woke to the irritating sound of a ringing phone. He leaned over the side of the futon mattress and reached for his jeans. Phone in hand, he flopped back on his pillow. "Hello?"

"Dr. Stanton, do you plan on joining the rest of the class for rounds? Or did you just assume you could stroll in anytime you felt like it?"

Eric shot straight up and looked at the clock. *Fuck!* "No, sir, uh, Dr. Peters. I'm sorry, I'll be there as soon as I can." He ended the call and jumped out of bed. Had he really slept for four hours? Felt more like one.

Eric kicked himself again when he couldn't find a pair of clean pants. He spun and began searching the floor of his room. "Ah ha," he declared victoriously as he held up a not-so-dirty pair of khakis.

After getting dressed, he made his way into the bathroom for a quick piss. Eric studied at himself in the mirror as he zipped up. "Holy crap," he mumbled, staring at his wayward blond curls. It looked like he had been in a wind tunnel. He picked up his hair brush and quickly wet as much of the thick locks as he could. "Come on, behave, you bastards."

Grabbing an apple from the makeshift kitchen counter, Eric ran out the door. The best perk to driving pizza deliveries for his uncle was getting to park right in front of the shop. He locked the door to his tiny apartment above 'Poppie's Pizza' and scrambled into his car.

As he pulled away from the curb, he bent across the console and opened the glove box, extracting a bottle of cologne. He didn't normally wear the stuff to the hospital, but without taking a shower, Eric knew he smelled like a greasy piece of pepperoni.

Eric took a bite of his apple as he drove north, out of Pacifica towards downtown San Francisco. He hated the drive, but what other choice did he have? The job working for his uncle not only paid for food and car insurance, but the majority of his rent as well. No way could he find that kind of deal in the city.

Of course having the long hours all medical interns enjoyed along with the part-time delivery gig, left little time for anything else, including sleep. At least he only had another six months on his internship. After that he would move up to a resident position. Unlike most medical students, Eric poured almost every cent of the small salary he earned as an intern into paying back his student loans. He'd already started to make a dent in the overwhelming amount, and he was hopeful he'd have the entire dollar figure paid off well before most guys in his class. It was a matter of pride with him. His family had refused to pay a cent towards his education, and Eric had discovered it meant more anyway to do it on his own.

Eric pulled into the employee parking lot, and grabbed his identification tag out of the console.

Rushing into the hospital, he stopped by his locker long enough to pull out his short white coat. By the time he reached the floor where his small group followed Dr. Peters on rounds, Eric was out of breath.

"How nice of you to join us, Dr. Stanton," Dr. Peters quipped, glancing over the tiny glasses perched on the end of his aquiline nose. Eric had often wondered how old his boss was. Although he could tell Dr. Peters' hair was prematurely grey, and he had the tiny-webbed wrinkles around his grey eyes, Eric guessed him to only be around forty-five.

Eric tried his best to spend the rest of the afternoon hiding behind his fellow interns. Six months, he kept repeating the words over and over in his head. He just prayed his body would hold out that long. It was getting to the point where he barely recognised himself when he looked into the mirror. Working twenty-four to forty-eight hour shifts at the hospital on top of the hours he picked up at Poppie's left virtually no time for food or sleep. He'd lost a lot of weight and it seemed the dark circles under his eyes were a permanent fixture. He usually got twenty-four hours off after a forty-eight hours shift, but he was still on-call. With budget cuts, he was called in eight times out of ten. Mondays were his day off from Poppie's, the only day he was blessed with more than two or three hours of sleep. *Just get me to Monday.*

* * * *

Zac glanced at the clock once again. Forty minutes. Damn. His stomach rumbled, reminding him he still hadn't eaten. "Just be patient," he admonished, looking down at his body. He grinned at the half-hard cock trapped behind the fly of his jeans. "Both of you."

Earlier in the week he'd ordered a pizza, hoping to see Eric again, but some other kid had shown up at the door. Zac had smoothly asked the driver where Eric was, and the guy had told him Eric worked some really fucked-up hours. Zac struck up a conversation with the kid and ended up giving him an extra fifty bucks if he'd get a copy of Eric's schedule and drop it by. Yeah, he knew it was pathetic, but he had thought of little else all week.

Zac glanced at the crumpled paper on the coffee table, Thursday ten to two. He shook his head. Who the hell orders pizza after midnight? Drunks and druggies, that's who. He didn't like the thought of Eric walking up to strange houses at that time of night.

"Oh, man, what the hell is wrong with me?" He'd never had it this bad for someone he'd barely met. Zac stood and walked to the window. Hell, he didn't even know if Eric was gay and there Zac was, weaving a future with him. Another glance at the clock, and his palms began to sweat. He turned on the outdoor lights and went to his bedroom. With the lights off, he knew he'd be able to see Eric pull up without being detected. Once again, he felt an "oooh" moment. *Am I really being this creepy?*

Zac vowed he'd have a serious talk with himself in the morning. He was an extremely successful high school football coach, smart, funny, pretty nice to look at, or so he'd been told, so why now? Why Eric?

A battered white Toyota Corolla pulled up in the drive. Zac held his breath as he gazed down at Eric through the windshield. Zac chuckled to himself as Eric appeared to be attacked by a case of the yawns before getting out of the car.

The door opened and Eric lifted out a Poppie's Pizza box. The man was even more gorgeous than Zac had remembered. Despite his wrinkled clothing and out-of-control curls, Eric looked more like a male model than a delivery guy.

Pulling away from the window, Zac hurried back into the living room when Eric started up the stairs. He quickly turned on the television so he didn't appear as pathetic as he really was. The bell rang and Zac counted to ten before getting up to answer.

Opening the door, Zac gazed at his little blond Adonis. "Hey, Eric," he greeted.

Eric stared at him like he was crazy. He glanced over his shoulder towards his car before turning back to Zac. "Umm, do we know each other?"

Zac felt like a loser. "No, not really. You delivered here on Saturday. Remember? I was having poker night? I told you my name was Zac and asked you yours?" *Please stop me before I make a complete ass out of myself.*

Then it happened. Eric's mouth turned up into the most devastating smile Zac had ever seen. "Sorry, man. I was just coming off a double shift at the hospital. I'd worked almost forty-eight straight before I started delivering."

"Hospital?"

"I'm six months into my internship, and yes, the hours are as bad as what they show on TV." Eric graced Zac with yet another smile. "I'm sorry, I don't remember your name."

"Zac. Zac Grainger." He knew it was now or never. "So, you like Chinese? I thought maybe we could meet for dinner some evening?"

Eric handed over the pizza and shook his head. "Sounds heavenly, but I don't have time for a social life, I'm a doctor," Eric proclaimed with a wink.

At least he hadn't turned up his nose at the idea of a date. Maybe things were looking up. "Surely you have to eat."

Eric chuckled and stared down at himself. "Does it look like I get much free time for such frivolous activities?"

Zac started to shake his head, but decided to press on. What did he have to lose? "You get days off?"

Eric bit his lip. "Not really. I'm supposed to, but I usually get called in. Although I don't deliver on Monday nights. But it's the only time I catch more than a couple hours of sleep."

"Mondays work for me," Zac spoke up, grasping at the chance to see Eric. "I could make you a nice home-cooked dinner. I promise not to keep you out late."

Eric appeared confused. "Why would you do that? I was serious when I said I didn't have time for a social life."

Zac shrugged. "I like you. Actually, you're probably the first person I've really been attracted to in years. It's just dinner." He held his breath as Eric seemed to contemplate the invitation.

"It'll be late. I don't get off shift until nine and it takes me about forty-five minutes to get down here from the city."

"That's fine. I'll have dinner ready at ten. You should be home before midnight." Zac felt like pumping his arms into the air.

Finally, Eric grinned and nodded. "I'd like that. Umm, you might need to call and remind me though. The weekends are usually pretty brutal and by Monday I can barely remember my own name."

Zac took a step back. "Let me set the pizza down and get a paper and pen." He hesitated to make sure Eric wasn't going to bolt as soon as he turned his back.

"Yeah, okay. That'll be sixteen-fifty-seven, by the way."

Shit, he'd almost forgot about paying for the pizza. "Sure, hang on."

Zac set the box on the coffee table and ran to the kitchen. Pulling out his junk drawer, he scrambled to find a pen that actually worked and a scrap of paper. "Sorry," he apologised coming back into the living room. "Why is it that pens seem to go dry overnight?"

Eric yawned, quickly covering his mouth. The action made Zac feel like a piece of shit. Eric was trying to be patient and there Zac was making stupid jokes. He tore the paper in half and scrawled his name and number on it, using the wall as a desk. "Okay, what's your number?"

Eric rattled off his cell number around another yawn. Zac shook his head. The poor guy was dead on his feet. He dug in his front pocket and came back with a twenty. He handed the money and his number to Eric. "I'll be looking forward to talking to you."

Eric glanced at the number in his hand. "Mind if I call you if I get a break from work?"

"No, not at all. I'd like that very much," Zac told him.

"Cool." Eric smiled and started walking down the steps. "Thanks, by the way."

"For what?" Zac asked, stepping out onto the landing.

"For actually giving me something to think about besides Mrs. Hopkins and her bed sores."

Zac chuckled. "My pleasure." He gave Eric one last wave as he pulled out of the driveway. He shut and locked the door and turned towards the pizza. He was sure it had to be cold by now. Zac crossed his fingers that Eric wouldn't get into trouble for spending fifteen minutes on one delivery.

He flopped down on the couch and opened the box. The grease was starting to congeal a bit on the top of the pepperoni, but it still looked good. Zac picked up a slice and devoured it in five bites. He'd have to ask Trey what he should make for Monday night's dinner. Trey was the only guy he hung with who knew anything about cooking, and Zac would definitely need a few pointers.

He briefly thought of calling his mom, but quickly decided against it. All jZac's mom needed was a mention of a man in Zac's life and she'd have them married by Christmas.

Pushing away the thoughts, Zac decided to concentrate on his upcoming date. He may only get to spend a few short hours in Eric's company, but he already knew it would be worth it.

* * * *

Zac was stuffing practice jerseys in the washing machine when Trey walked in. "You wanted to see me?" Trey asked, jumping up to sit on the dryer.

After a glance around the equipment room to make sure they were alone, Zac shut the washer lid and nodded. "I need your help. I'm making dinner for a new guy and don't have a clue what to fix."

Trey's pale green eyes sparkled with interest. "Tell me more about this guy."

Zac crossed his arms and leaned his hip against the washer. "I don't really know much other than he's a doctor, intern actually. He's the guy who delivered the pizzas the other night."

"Seriously? A doctor making house calls?" Trey joked, his light brown-coloured skin crinkling around his eyes.

"I like him," Zac stated simply, squashing any further barbs from his buddy.

Trey rubbed his jaw. "Well, if he's working at Poppie's, you know Italian's out."

"I told him it would be a home-cooked meal and his mouth practically watered," Zac added.

Trey threw up his hands. "Oh, you should've said that. You can't go wrong with pot roast. It's easy enough even you can manage it."

"Har, har," Zac quipped, giving Trey a playful shove.

The gesture almost knocked Trey off the dryer. "Sorry," Zac apologised. He forgot how frail Trey was for a guy. Zac was used to being around athletes. Trey was the only man he'd ever hung out with who was more likely to be in the band than on the field. The thought of Trey with a flute in his hand had him chuckling.

"What?" Trey asked defensively.

"Did you play an instrument in school?"

"Yeah, why?"

Zac barely restrained his smile. "Just wondering."

Trey hopped off the dryer and started towards the door. "I can come over on Sunday and we can go to the grocery store if you want?"

"Sounds good." Zac's cell phone started playing *Let's Get it On* by Marvin Gaye. His heart nearly stopped at the song he'd programmed in along with Eric's number. He pulled the phone out of his short's pocket and walked towards his office. "Hey, Eric," he answered.

"Hi. I hope I'm not calling at a bad time?"

"No, not at all. I'm just messing around in the equipment room waiting for practice to start." He sat in his desk chair and put his feet up on the scarred wooden surface.

"Huh? You're an athlete or something?"

Zac chuckled. "Yes and no. I'm a high school football coach here in town."

"Oh," Eric replied. "My dad was a football coach."

"Was? Did he pass away?" Zac hated the hurt he detected in Eric's voice.

"Uh, no. I mean, he still may be coaching. Truthfully I don't really know."

"I'm sorry to hear that. Is it because you came out?" Zac asked.

Eric snorted. "That along with a few other things, but I don't want to talk about him."

Zac knew when to back off. No sense scaring Eric away before their first date. "So, you at the hospital?"

"Yeah. It's a slow day in the ER, thank God. I'm supposed to be taking my lunch break, but I forgot to bring anything again, so I thought I'd give you a call."

"You're not eating? Damn. I wish I was closer. I'd be more than happy to bring you something." Zac hated the idea of Eric not taking care of himself.

"Thanks. It's been a long time since someone's given a damn whether I ate or not."

"I definitely give a damn."

Eric sputtered for a few seconds. "Um, I'm looking forward to dinner. I know I asked you to call and remind me, but I don't think that'll be necessary. Actually, I've thought of little else."

Warmth wormed its way into Zac's chest. "Me, too. I was starting to think there was something wrong with me. I haven't looked so forward to anything in years, many years."

Eric's sneeze took Zac by surprise, making him jump. "Bless you.".

"Thanks. I think I'm getting a cold or something. Goes with the territory," Eric answered. "Hang on a sec." Zac heard Eric put the phone down and blow his nose. "Sorry about that."

"No problem. You know you'd probably feel a lot better if you ate something." Great. Now he sounded like a mother hen.

"I will. Uncle Lewis usually feeds me before my shift."

"Uncle Lewis?"

"Poppie from Poppie's Pizza. He's my mom's brother. Lewis gives me a place to stay above the pizza shop for next to nothing and dinner every night in exchange for working as many hours as I can manage."

"He doesn't pay you?" Zac was appalled. No wonder Eric didn't have money to buy himself something to eat.

"I keep my tips. Believe me, what he gives in the way of food and shelter is more than I could afford if he paid me. It's a good trade."

"I thought interns got paid. Why do you need two jobs?"

There was a slight pause on Eric's end. "I get a small salary, which is really a joke considering the hours I put in, but I try to use it for other things."

"Other things?"

"Loan payments. I think the hardest part of medical school is knowing how much money you're racking up in student loans. I decided that since I didn't have time for a life anyway right now, it made sense to pay off as much as I could."

Zac was impressed and appalled at the same time. He knew the kind of hours med students put in, and made a mental note to tip Eric more the next time he delivered.

Zac heard a commotion in the background a second before Eric spoke. "Sorry, gotta go. Traffic accident."

"Okay. Call when you get another break." Zac hated to hang up, but he also knew the kids were probably out on the field waiting for him.

"I will. Thanks for letting me bug you."

"Are you kidding? This has been the highlight of my day," Zac told him honestly.

"Good, mine too."

Eric hung up and Zac pocketed his phone. As he walked towards the field, he rubbed his chest. The warmth of emotion was a new and exciting feeling.

Chapter Three

Zac felt much better after a shower. He thought about going to bed, but knew he'd just end up tossing and turning. Man it sucked to lose and break their winning streak. Zac hoped his players would take the loss and learn from it. If they had hopes of going to the playoffs, they'd need to win their next two games.

He slipped on a pair of sweats, and pulled a beer out of the fridge when the doorbell rang. Zac glanced at the clock, surprised it was already eleven. He set his beer on the coffee table and answered the door.

Eric stood on the landing holding a pizza box. "Thought you could use something to eat."

Zac smiled, more than pleased at the unexpected visit. "Come in," he greeted, stepping back.

Eric grinned and followed Zac into the apartment. "I heard about the loss on the radio."

Zac realised he didn't care anymore about the loss, especially with Eric standing in his apartment. He took the pizza and set it on the table. "Thanks for thinking of me." God, he wanted to pull Eric into his arms. He'd thought of nothing except the man in front of him for an entire week and had yet to even hold him.

Eric glanced around the room. "Well, I should probably go," he mumbled.

Zac knew it was now or never. Something was needed to break the ice between them. He walked up to Eric and wrapped his arms around the smaller man. Eric surprised him by snuggling even further into Zac's embrace. Closing his eyes, Zac rested his cheek against the top of Eric's head. "This feels nice," he whispered.

Eric nuzzled his face against Zac's bare chest. "Too nice. It's, uh, been a long time," Eric confessed.

When Eric's lips brushed across Zac's nipple an involuntary moan escaped him. "Tell me you can stay?" He bent to whisper against Eric's mouth.

Fingers curled around the back of Zac's head as they began to kiss. Eric's tongue brushing against his had Zac rock hard in no time. The kiss was the most erotic foreplay Zac had ever experienced. He slid his hands down to cup Eric's small ass and lifted. His soon-to-be lover didn't even hesitate before wrapping his legs around Zac's waist.

With the man of his dreams in his arms, Zac turned and steadied Eric against the closest wall. Their tongues continued to duel as Zac ground the hard length of his cock against the prominent ridge in Eric's jeans. "Need you," Zac groaned, as they came up for air.

Eric's brown eyes met Zac's. "You have no idea how good that sounds, but I have to get back to work." Eric went from a moan to a chuckle when Zac began dry humping him. "And delivering pizzas with dried cum all over myself is not exactly the way I want to spend my Friday night."

Zac reluctantly stilled his hips. "Monday can't get here soon enough."

Eric kissed Zac again, nipping his bottom lip before he pulled back. "Maybe I can get someone to fill in for me for a few hours. Lord knows I've done enough of it for them."

Eric kicked his legs free and Zac lowered him to the floor. "I get home around six-thirty." Eric nodded and adjusted the erection trapped behind his zipper. Damn, Zac wanted to do that for him.

"Can I call you?" Eric asked, opening the apartment door.

"Every chance you get." Zac ran his knuckles down the side of Eric's face. He was pleased when Eric closed his eyes and leaned into the touch. Zac took the opportunity to lean down for one more kiss.

When the kiss threatened to become explosive once again, Zac stepped back. "You'd better go before I strip you naked right here where we stand."

Eric grinned. "Rain check?"

"Definitely."

Eric stepped onto the landing and openly ogled Zac's tented sweats. "Yeah, definitely."

With an exaggerated groan, Zac shut the door. The minute he heard Eric's car fire up and pull out of the drive, Zac pushed his hand down the front of his pants and wrapped his fingers around his cock.

He gathered pre-cum from the head and used it to set up a quick rhythm. Christ Almighty what was he going to do until Monday?

* * * *

The following afternoon, Zac sprawled on the couch watching college football, hand down his sweats, idly playing with his cock. He'd jerked off four times since the episode with Eric and still didn't feel sated.

A loud knock at the door startled him. The thought that it was Eric delivering him another surprise pizza, had the cock in his hand straining to break out of his pants. The scuffling and arguing behind the closed door quickly told him it wasn't Eric. With a chuckle, he removed the hold on his erection and rose to answer the door.

"Hey," he greeted and turned to go back to the couch. Zac sat in the corner and put a pillow over his lap to hide his hard-on.

Bobby, Marco and Kent walked into the living room, each of them carrying a six-pack. "Thought we'd watch the games with you," Kent declared, taking a chair and opening a beer.

"You mean you thought I'd be depressed because of the loss and wanted to cheer me up," Zac corrected.

Kent grinned. "That too."

"Well I'm fine, but you're more than welcome to stay."

Bobby kicked off his athletic shoes and stretched out on the couch, using the pillow in Zac's lap to rest his head on. "Make yourself at home, Bobby," Zac chuckled.

"Always do," Bobby replied, reaching to the floor for a beer.

"Sooo, tell us why you aren't all suicidal over your first defeat of the season?" Marco asked, sitting across from Kent in the only other chair.

Zac shrugged, and reached down to play with Bobby's dark brown hair. "I don't know. I was in a shitty mood when I got home and then Eric dropped by to deliver a pizza, and I haven't really given it much thought since."

Bobby turned his head away from the game to glance up at Zac. "Eric? Do tell!"

"He delivered the pizzas on poker night. We've kinda hit it off since then." Zac wasn't sure why he felt uncomfortable talking to his friends about Eric, maybe because he'd never talked about anyone with the guys.

Bobby seemed to study Zac for several moments. "You've got it bad, don't you?"

Zac tried to deny it. "We haven't even officially gone out yet. He's coming over Monday night for a late dinner after his shift at the hospital."

"And the plot thickens," Marco said. "What does your young man do at the hospital?"

"He's an intern." Zac sighed, deciding to give up the fight for privacy. He knew his friends would continue to badger him until they knew everything anyway. "He works crazy hours at the hospital and then delivers pizza for his uncle in exchange for room, board and tips. He's about five-foot-nine, blond curly hair, the prettiest brown eyes I've ever seen and the softest lips I've ever tasted."

Bobby smiled and bounced his head against the pillow in Zac's lap. "Down boy." He chuckled and batted his long lashes at Zac. "Does he have prettier eyes than me?"

"Oh get out," Marco cut in. "Everyone knows I've got the best eyes of the group."

Zac chuckled. Marco's lashes were longer than any woman's, and the colour so dark brown they appeared black. Kent snorted, shaking his head. That made Zac's chuckle turn into a full-blown laugh. "Why don't you two just fuck and get it over with."

Kent's jaw dropped in surprise, but Zac noticed the wistful expression on Marco's face. "Sorry," Zac apologised. "Just trying to take some of the spotlight off my burgeoning relationship."

"Relationship?" Bobby whistled. "Moving kinda fast, aren't you?"

Zac shrugged. "I don't know where it'll go, if anywhere, but it feels different." He was saved from further explanations when his cell phone began playing the Marvin Gaye tune. Zac quickly reached for it, much to the delight of his friends.

"Oh, you are so gonna be teased for that choice," Marco laughed.

"Shut up." Zac opened his phone. "Hey, can you hold on a second?"

"Sure," Eric answered.

Zac extricated himself from Bobby's head and stood. "I'm gonna take this in the bedroom," he told his friends.

Bobby reached out and playfully slapped the tented fabric of Zac's sweats. "Yeah, I'd say that was a good idea."

Embarrassed as hell, Zac walked into his bedroom and shut the door. "Okay, sorry about that. A few of my friends are over to watch the games."

"Oh," Eric said. "Go be with your friends. I didn't really want anything..."

"No. I'd much rather talk to you. So, on a break?" Zac propped pillows against his headboard and leaned back.

"Yeah. Well, more like between emergencies."

"I can't stop thinking about you," Zac admitted, pushing his left hand under the waistband of his sweats.

"Me either," Eric admitted. "It's your fault my pants aren't fitting as well these days."

Zac sighed. "Join the club. It doesn't seem to matter how many cold showers I take, or how many times I jack-off. The second you come to mind, my dick goes hard." He rested the phone between his ear and shoulder leaving his right hand free to fondle and squeeze his balls.

Eric groaned. "You're not making this any easier. I'm surrounded by a room full of people."

Zac grinned, deciding to torture Eric even further. "So I shouldn't tell you that I can't wait to lick every inch of that sweet little butt of yours?"

Eric whimpered and Zac knew he had him. "I can't stop thinking about what the inside of your ass tastes like. I wanna stick my tongue as far into you as possible. Then I'm gonna fuck you until I'm imprinted on your soul for the rest of your life."

He heard Eric's breathing increase. Zac jerked himself faster, pushing a finger into his own hole. "I'm fingering my ass. Do you like that? Would you like to touch me there?"

"Yessss," Eric hissed.

"Would you like me to touch you there?"

"God, yes," Eric panted.

The need in Eric's voice sent Zac over the edge, growling his soon-to-be lover's name. He dropped the phone as his body convulsed with his release. "Hang on," he managed to get out. He fumbled for the phone and put it back to his ear. Eric's whimpers were heard loud and clear.

"You're an evil man, Zac Grainger."

"Next time call from the bathroom and we can both get off." Zac rubbed the cum into his stomach.

"Believe me, I will. I think the people around me think I'm sick or something with all the moaning I've been doing," Eric chuckled.

"I may just need to order a pizza later. I miss those lips."

"And they miss you," Eric whispered. "I need to get back. Maybe I'll see you for a few minutes later?"

"Count on it." Zac hung up the phone and reached for the towel beside his bed. After wiping his stomach clean, he pulled up his sweats and walked out of his room. Instead of going back into the living room, he ducked into the bathroom. If the guys smelled spunk on him, he'd never live it down.

After a quick wash in the sink, Zac rejoined his friends. He noticed none of them acknowledged his return, but they all had shit-eating grins on their faces.

Bobby sat up and Zac resumed their earlier position. "Everything come out okay?" Bobby finally chuckled.

"Yep," Zac answered, refusing to give them anymore fodder.

* * * *

When the doorbell rang later that night, Zac pounced. He knew he didn't have much time and he wanted everything he could get. He quickly opened the door and pulled Eric inside, relieving him of the pizza.

After stuffing a twenty and a five into Eric's front jeans pocket, he let his hands wander, as he dove in for a kiss. His hands weren't the only ones exploring. Eric went a step further and slipped his down below Zac's waistband.

"Aaahh," Zac moaned, when he felt Eric's hand on his cock for the first time.

Eric broke the kiss and fell to his knees in front of Zac. "Need to taste you." Eric stared up at Zac through long blond lashes. "Are you safe?" he asked, before running his tongue up Zac's length.

"Yeah." Knowing time was of the essence, Zac reached down and pulled Eric to his feet. "Let's do this together."

Eric appeared confused for a second before a lecherous grin spread across his face. "Lead the way," he said, unfastening his jeans.

By the time they reached the couch, they were both naked from the waist down. Zac was surprised by not only the length, but the girth of Eric's cock. He couldn't wait to get his lips around such a thing of beauty.

Being the bigger man, Zac stretched out on the sofa and positioned Eric in the typical sixty-nine position over him. After his first taste of Eric's pre-cum, he knew he'd be an addict for life.

When Eric's lips encased the head of his cock, Zac thought he'd come on the spot. Damn, the man knew how to suck. He released the cock in his mouth to slide his tongue down the length to Eric's sac, taking his balls one at a time into his mouth. Eric's increasing moans let him know his lover was definitely thinking about their phone conversation earlier.

Without preamble, Zac released Eric's balls and zeroed in on that sweet hole. He used both hands to separate those cute little cheeks and buried his face in the crack of Eric's ass, his tongue already probing the tight pucker.

Eric released Zac's cock and repositioned, giving Zac even more room to play. After licking the tight ring of muscles, it began to relax and loosen. Zac took advantage and pushed his thumb as deep inside Eric's body as it would go.

"Fuck," Eric cried, back bowing.

Once he moved in and out of Eric's ass with ease, Zac removed his thumb and replaced it with his tongue.

"Oh, God, I'm gonna come," Eric panted, riding Zac's face.

Although Zac wanted to swallow every ounce of cum Eric's cock produced, his busy tongue had other ideas. He continued to eat Eric's ass until the muscles contracted around his tongue. Eric rode out his orgasm while still sitting on Zac's face which was fine by him.

Zac couldn't wait to replace his tongue with his cock. He didn't know if he'd ever fucked a more responsive lover. The thought of burying himself balls deep inside Eric's ass, had his balls drawing up tight. "Gonna come," he shouted.

Eric fell forward and swallowed as much of Zac's cock as he could. The welcoming heat pushed Zac over the edge, erupting in stream after stream of seed. Just when he thought he was finished, Eric pressed his tongue into the slit on Zac's crown, and he rewarded his lover with another shot of his essence.

Zac reached between them and ran his fingers through Eric's cum, which had landed on his chest. Sucking the thick fluid from his fingers, Zac moaned. He glanced at the clock. Eric had already been there for fifteen minutes. "Hope you don't have pizzas in the car, or they'll be cold by the time you deliver them."

Eric chuckled and turned around to straddle Zac's chest. After leaning down for a deep kiss he sighed. "No, I made sure you were my last delivery, but I need to get back. I'm sure Uncle Lewis has more."

"What time do you have to go into the hospital in the morning?"

"Six," Eric groaned and stood up.

Zac took the opportunity to lean up on his elbow and lick the few spots of cum that had splashed onto Eric's stomach. "You could always come back here after work. I'd make sure you wake up in time for the hospital in the morning." He hated the thought of Eric leaving him.

"I can't. By the time I get to bed I'll be lucky to get three hours of sleep as it is." Eric pulled on his underwear and jeans. He sat on the edge of the couch and tied his shoelaces. "Sorry. I know my schedule sucks. It's the reason I've shied away from dating."

Zac ran his hand up Eric's spine. "We'll work it out." He pulled Eric down for one last kiss. "You're worth the wait."

Chapter Four

Zac was waiting for Eric at the top of the stairs when his car pulled in the drive. He'd never admit it, but he needed the fresh night air to keep him awake. How in the hell did Eric keep such late hours day after day?

"Hey," Eric greeted, bottle of wine in hand.

"As much as I want to kiss you, I think we should go inside." Zac stood and opened the door. He wasn't a prude exactly, but making out in full view of the family he rented from wasn't his idea of appropriate. The Collingers were damn nice people. He knew they could probably get a lot more for the apartment he rented, but they said they liked the idea of a teacher living close. Zac still didn't know what that meant. Yeah, he was a teacher, but he was also a single gay man. They didn't seem to have a problem with his sexual orientation, which was a damn good thing, because right then he wanted nothing more than to fuck his new lover all night long.

Zac noticed the yawn as Eric stepped into the living room. "Tired?" Zac asked. *Duh, of course he's tired.*

"I'm okay," Eric answered, handing Zac the wine bottle. "The lady at the store said it would go with just about anything."

"It will. Thanks." Zac led the way into the kitchen. "I have everything ready except the gravy. I hope you like pot roast?"

Eric grinned. "I love it. I haven't had it in years."

Zac set the wine down and pulled Eric in for a kiss. Just before their mouths touched, Eric let out another yawn. "Sorry," Eric chuckled.

"Don't apologise." Zac gave Eric the kiss he'd been dying to give him since the moment he left Saturday night. He pulled back and grinned. "Have a seat. The gravy shouldn't take long."

Zac pulled the roast from the oven and stuck a fork in the potatoes and carrots to make sure they were well cooked. Confident that he'd done a decent job, he spooned the vegetables into a large serving bowl before lifting the roast out of the pan. He sent up a quick prayer he'd remembered everything Trey had taught him the previous day.

"How're things at the hospital?" he asked, mixing cornstarch and cold water into a glass.

"Okay. It's flu season, so we see a lot of puking kids this time of year." Eric shuddered. "Sorry, guess that's not a very good topic right before dinner," he chuckled. "I really need to work on my social skills."

Zac whisked the mixture into the pan of roast broth. "I'm the one who asked." He thought of how depressing it must be to work in an emergency room day in and day out. "Does it get to you? Ya know, the death and stuff?"

Eric covered a yawn. "Sometimes, but I think it's better than some of the other medical fields. Usually our patients are in and out. We don't really have time to form any kind of bond with them. It makes it easier, I think."

Zac scrutinised his gravy, a few lumps, but not bad for a first effort. He poured the gravy into a bowl and took it to the table along with the rest of the food. "Will you open the wine?" he asked, handing the bottle and a corkscrew to Eric.

"So, what made you want to become a doctor?" Zac pulled two wine glasses out of the cabinet and surveyed them for dust. It wasn't often that he drank wine, but he was glad Eric had brought it.

Eric waited for Zac to take his seat. "First off, let me tell you how much I appreciate this. Not many guys would go to this much trouble at ten o'clock at night."

Zac leaned over the corner of the table and gave Eric a kiss. "I'm not most guys, and neither are you."

Eric smiled and nodded. He began talking as they filled their plates. "When I was young, it seemed I spent most of my time in the emergency room with one injury or another."

Zac's heart skipped a beat. He reached for Eric's hand. "Were you…abused?"

Eric looked confused for a moment, before a chuckle escaped him. "God, no. Nothing like that." Eric ate a piece of roast. "Mmm, this is fantastic."

"Thanks," Zac acknowledged the compliment.

"I've already told you my dad was a coach."

"Yeah."

"Well, he wanted a jock for a son." Eric took another bite of food. "He deserved it, too, but instead he got me. Oh, I tried, I really did. Dad had me tossing a football with him in the yard before I was even in school."

Eric shrugged and speared a carrot onto his fork. "My body just wasn't built for football. I had a lot of injuries, even more when I was in high school."

"And he still insisted you play?" Zac couldn't believe a father could be so selfish. Didn't he realise what a remarkable son he had?

"We didn't really discuss whether I would or wouldn't, it was a given. I'm still not sure if I felt sorry for him, or if I was just trying to make him proud." Eric seemed to contemplate his feelings as he chewed. "Dad was a really big deal in my town. What must it have been like to have a wimp for a son."

"So you were an only child?"

"No. I have a sister." Eric snorted. "Jeanie's probably a lot stronger than I am, but...ya know." Eric shrugged.

Zac's heart was breaking for the young man who'd tried to live up to his dad's reputation. "So when did you decide on medicine?"

"I think I always knew it was what I wanted to do, but it wasn't until my senior year that I told my folks. Dad was pushing me to attend the local junior college so I could continue to play football, but I wanted to go to Stanford. I'd worked damn hard in school to get the grades for it. I didn't want to go to a junior college just to play football, especially because I knew I wasn't good enough, so I told them."

The fact that Eric hadn't talked to his father in a while gave Zac a clue as to how they took it. "How did they react?"

Eric took a drink of his wine. "They didn't. Dad told me if I was too good to go to junior college I could damn well pay for Stanford myself." Eric set his glass down. "So I am. I guess that's part of the reason I'm obsessed with paying down my loans."

"And because of that you haven't spoken to them?"

"No. It wasn't just my choice of college that divided us. The gay thing had a lot to do with it as well. I just wasn't what my dad wanted. We tried a couple of times, but things were strained. My mom couldn't deal with being in the middle, so she eventually left my dad, which only made things worse between him and me." Eric shrugged again. "It's okay. I don't blame anyone."

Zac finished his food. He noticed how little Eric actually ate. Zac wondered if the food hadn't been to Eric's liking or if he always ate so little. "You finished?" Zac asked, gesturing to Eric's plate.

"Yes, thank you." Eric rubbed his stomach. "I can't remember a time when I've eaten so much. I'm going to be full for a week."

Zac paused in the process of picking up Eric's plate. He hated to sound like Eric's father, but dammit, his lover needed to eat more. Zac took the plates to the sink. "I've got a ton of roast left. Mind if I make up some sandwiches or something and send them home with you?"

"You don't have to do that."

"I don't *have* to do anything. But if I don't send some of this home with you, I'll end up throwing part of it away." *Please say yes.*

"Okay, that would be nice."

"Why don't you go relax in the living room? I'll just be a few minutes. I'm gonna leave the dishes for later."

Eric stood and walked over to Zac. "You're being awfully nice to me," Eric teased, wrapping his arms around Zac's waist.

"I like being nice to you," Zac answered back.

Eric ran his hands up Zac's chest to rest on his collar bone. "Be careful. I could get very used to letting someone take care of me the way you do."

Zac bent to kiss the man he was starting to fall for. "I hope so. It's all part of my devious plan to make sure you can't live without me."

* * * *

"Eric?" He heard someone whisper. "Eric, honey, it's time to wake up."

Eric opened his eyes. Zac sat on the floor resting his chin on his hands in front of Eric's face. Eric stretched. The couch had been so comfortable he must've fallen asleep. "Sorry. You should've nudged me earlier." Damn. He couldn't believe he'd done that after Zac had gone to all the trouble of making him such a fantastic meal.

"You evidently needed the sleep more than my company," Zac teased. "It's okay. I enjoyed watching you."

Eric hoped he hadn't drooled or farted in his sleep. That would be humiliating. "What time is it?"

"A few minutes after midnight. The offer still stands if you want to sack out here. I can set the alarm for whatever time you need to be up."

Eric studied the green eyes of the kindest man he'd ever dated. What had he ever done to deserve Zac Grainger? "I'd like that."

Zac's smile could have lit up the entire west coast. He stood and scooped Eric into his arms. "I can walk," Eric chuckled.

"I know." Zac deposited Eric in the centre of a large bed. "You get under the covers, and I'll put your sandwiches in the fridge and lock up."

Eric nodded and pulled his shirt over his head. Zac watched him for a few seconds before giving a shake to his head and walking out. Eric quickly stripped out of the rest of his clothes and climbed under the covers. *Oh, oh, damn.* The bed was a lot more comfortable than his hard futon.

By the time Zac joined him, Eric was almost asleep again. He curled against Zac's body and sighed. "I could get used to this."

"That's what I'm hoping," Zac whispered, kissing the top of Eric's head. "Sleep."

Eric nuzzled his face against Zac's chest until he found the perfect spot. *Yeah, I could definitely get used to this.*

* * * *

A vibration in Zac's pocket startled him. Laughing at himself, he pulled the phone out and glanced at the display. "Take over for me for a couple minutes," he told one of his assistant coaches.

Zac walked far enough away he wouldn't be overheard. "Hey," he answered.

"Did I catch you at a bad time?" Eric asked, sniffing.

"No. What's wrong?" he could tell his lover had either been crying or was sick.

"Just needed to talk to you. It's been a bad day."

"What happened?" Zac climbed the bleachers and sat half-way up.

"I lost a little girl. She'd been hit by a car on her way to school." Eric hiccupped around tears and Zac closed his eyes. He wished he were there to hold his lover.

"She wasn't stable when they brought her in, but I should've been able to save her. I've gone over and over it in my head. There had to have been something I did wrong."

"Oh, honey, please don't do this to yourself." Zac wiped a tear from his cheek. He wasn't sure if he was crying for the loss of the child or the pain in Eric's voice.

"Dr. Peters said I did everything right, but I just can't accept that," Eric went on.

Zac made a spur of the moment decision. "Can you get a break in about fifty minutes?"

Eric sniffed again. "I'm not sure. It depends on the work load. Why?"

"I'm going to bring you something for dinner."

"You don't have to do that. I ate the last of the roast sandwiches earlier."

"Actually, that was just an excuse to see you. I'll show up. If you can get a moment, great. If you can't, that's okay, too."

"What about practice?" Eric asked, but Zac heard the hope in his lover's voice.

"It's almost over anyway. Besides, I've got assistants who can handle it. I'll be there as soon as I can fight my way through the traffic."

"Okay. Um...thanks," Eric sighed.

Zac ended the call and after speaking to his defensive coach, ran to his jeep. As he wove his way through the evening traffic, he couldn't get the pain he'd heard in Eric's voice out of his head.

By the time he pulled into the parking lot, forty minutes had elapsed since he'd last spoken to Eric. He entered through the automatic doors and walked to the emergency desk.

"May I help you?" a young woman in pink scrubs asked.

"Is Dr. Stanton available?"

"Is this in regards to an emergency?"

Zac shook his head. "It's personal. I need to speak with him. If you could please tell him Zac Grainger is here to see him I'd appreciate it."

The woman eyed him warily for a few seconds. Zac didn't blame her. As a matter of fact, he appreciated her apprehension. "Hang on," she replied and picked up the phone. She spoke low enough that Zac couldn't hear her conversation above the activity in the waiting room behind him. Hanging up, she smiled. "Dr. Peters would like to speak with you. He'll be out in a moment."

Shit. Zac recognised the name of Eric's boss. He hoped like hell he hadn't gotten Eric into trouble by showing up. Zac nodded and stood to the side.

An older gentleman strode through the doors marked *Authorised Personnel Only* and spoke to the nurse at the desk. She pointed towards Zac and the doctor walked over. "Mr. Grainger?"

"Yes," Zac acknowledged.

The man stuck out his hand. "Doctor Jules Peters."

"Nice to meet you, Dr. Peters. I hope I haven't overstepped the rules or anything by showing up."

"No, not at all. As a matter of fact, I'm glad Dr. Stanton has someone to lean on at a time like this." Dr. Peters led Zac to a small room off to the side of the waiting area. "Have a seat."

"Is something wrong?" Zac asked.

Dr. Peters seemed to weigh his words before speaking. "The death of a patient is never easy. Unfortunately, in this line of work, we see it far too often. Dr. Stanton isn't dealing well with this particular death. He's lost patients in the past, we all have, but this particular loss seems to be hitting him more than it should."

"He said she was a little girl," Zac reminded the doctor. Who wouldn't be upset?

"Yes, but unfortunately children do sometimes die." Dr. Peters rubbed his jaw. "I think it would benefit everyone involved if Dr. Stanton took a few days off. I'd like for him to talk to one of our grief counsellors on staff here at the hospital."

"Do you think seeing a counsellor is really necessary?"

"Yes." Dr. Peters paused before continuing. "I've been doing this job for a number of years, and occasionally a student…shuts down after an event like this. They drop out of the programme because they begin to believe they weren't meant to be a doctor after all. I see those signs in Dr. Stanton, and I'd like to intervene on his behalf. He's a hell of a doctor, probably one of the finest students I've ever worked with as a matter of fact."

"What can I do?"

"Make sure he gets some sleep. Listen to him." Dr. Peters studied Zac for several moments. Zac was sure he was trying to figure out what kind of relationship the two of them had. "Be there for him. Encourage him to seek the counselling I'm suggesting."

"How long do you want him off work?"

"As long as it takes for him to understand we aren't gods, and we occasionally lose good people. It's human to feel bad, but a doctor cannot survive in this business if he takes death personally."

Zac nodded. "Where's Eric now?"

"I believe he's still in the restroom in the doctor's lounge. I'll take you there."

Zac stood and followed the doctor through the *Authorised Personnel Only* door, and down a hallway. "I'll sign him out," Dr. Peters informed Zac, gesturing towards the restroom door.

"Thank you," Zac said, shaking Dr. Peters' hand.

"Just do what you can. We need him around here." Dr. Peters winked before leaving the room.

Zac pushed open the door. "Eric?" He heard Eric sniffle a moment before blowing his nose.

The stall door opened and Eric walked straight into Zac's open arms. "I don't know what's wrong with me," Eric cried, his voice breaking.

Zac knew a lot of Eric's emotions were caused by the gruelling schedule and lack of proper meals. He also knew that wasn't what Eric needed to hear. "Why don't you let me take you to my place?"

"I can't. I have to work."

Zac held Eric in a protective embrace. "Dr. Peters has already signed you out. He thinks you need some time off to regroup."

Eric pulled back, his eyes red and swollen. "Am I in trouble?"

"Not at all," Zac answered, pulling Eric back against his chest. "He just wants to give you time to get over this." Zac gave Eric a quick kiss. "Come on. We can talk more later."

"You don't have to do this, you know."

Zac stopped walking and gazed into Eric's eyes. "I really wish you'd stop saying that. I know I don't have to do it. I've told you before and I'm sure I'll probably tell you again. I want to do this. I want to give you everything you need. I've never had anyone in my life that makes me feel the way you do. Indulge me. Please?"

Eric wiped his nose on a tissue. "Well, since you put it that way."

Zac chuckled and kissed him. "Come on."

Chapter Five

Zac glanced over to the sleeping man curled against the car door. He reached out and ran a hand over his shoulder. "Eric? We're almost home. I'm gonna drive through and get a burger, you want one?"

Eric rubbed his eyes and nodded. "Yeah, that sounds good." Eric yawned and glanced at his watch. "I've got to work in a couple hours."

Zac ground his teeth together to keep from barking orders like he did with his football players. "If Dr. Peters thinks you should take a few days off, I think you should listen to him."

Eric reached over and placed his hand on Zac's thigh. "I think taking some time away from the hospital is a good idea, but Uncle Lewis is counting on me. I'll be delivering pizzas, not trying to save lives."

"You need sleep," Zac reminded Eric.

"And I promise to get it after my shift."

Zac shut his mouth as he pulled into his favourite burger joint. He wasn't giving up his position on

Eric's second job, but he knew it wasn't the time. If he didn't back off, Eric would dig his heels in and Zac would never convince him. "What sounds good?" he asked, looking at the menu board. "Their chilli-cheese dogs are fantastic if you like that sort of thing."

"That sounds fine, no onion." Eric grinned. "I hope to do a little kissing later."

Zac's cock twitched in excitement. He placed their order and pulled around to the drive-up window. After putting the jeep into park, he pulled out his wallet. When he spotted Eric doing the same, he shook his head. "I got it. You can pay for the next one," he added.

Eric sighed and put his wallet away. "I'm going to hold you to that."

Zac chuckled. "I hope you will. That means I get at least one more date." He took the food from the woman and handed it over to Eric. "I didn't get any drinks, got plenty of those at home."

He heard a sack crinkle as he pulled back onto the street and moments later a fry touched his lips. With a smile, Zac opened his mouth and accepted the hot salty fried potato. "Mmm, damn they have good fries."

Eric seemed to agree, humming around his own fry. Zac studied Eric from the corner of his eye. He couldn't help but wonder if his lover's lighter mood was because of him, or if Eric suppressed his feelings for Zac's sake.

He parked in front of his apartment and something dawned on him. "If you're going to insist on delivering pizzas later, you'll have to use my jeep."

"Shit, I hadn't thought of that." Eric thumped his head against the seat. "Do you mind?"

"Hell no. It means you'll have to come back here after you get done." Zac decided to take it further. "Course I'll probably be too tired to drive you home, so you'll just have to plan on staying the night."

"It'll be late. You sure it's okay?"

Zac got out of the jeep and waited for Eric. As soon as his lover joined him, Zac wrapped an arm around Eric's waist. "More than okay. I know it hasn't even been two weeks, but I've thought of nothing else but getting you in my bed." He leaned over and kissed Eric's temple. "You might bring a change or two of clothes back with you."

Zac unlocked the front door and led the way into the kitchen. "What would you like to drink? I've got pop, beer, juice…"

"Water's fine," Eric said, getting their food out of the bag.

Zac fixed Eric a glass of ice water and grabbed a beer for himself. "I have an away game tomorrow, so it'll be close to eleven before I get home. Will you be here?"

Eric took a bite of his chilli-dog and shook his head. "I'll need to work. Maybe I can find someone to take me into the hospital to pick up my car."

Picking up his burger, Zac studied the thick beef patty. He didn't want Eric to have access to his car just yet. Call him selfish, but Zac liked the thought of Eric being at his house. If Eric got his car back, he wouldn't have the need to stay the night. "That's not necessary. I'll come home for lunch and you can run me back up to the school."

"How will you get home?" Eric asked.

"I'm sure at least one of my friends will be at the game. They're pretty good about supporting me that way." Damn, that reminded him. "I hope you don't mind, but Saturday night is poker night. I've got a group of five friends that come over every other week. You're more than welcome to join us."

Eric ate another french fry. "We'll see. I'm not sure if I'll be working at the hospital by then. I have a feeling all I need is a really good night's sleep."

Zac had serious doubts about that, but he held his tongue. He finished his food and beer, slyly watching Eric. In the end, Eric managed to finish about half of his food. "You want me to wrap that up for later?"

Eric shook his head and rubbed his stomach. "No. I'm not sure how well it's going to set with me as it is."

"You didn't like it?"

"I loved it. Maybe it's all the Italian food I've been eating lately, but my stomach hasn't been dealing with the spicy stuff very well."

"You could be getting an ulcer." Zac rolled up their trash and placed it back in the paper sack before throwing the whole thing in the waste basket. He got another beer out of the fridge and turned to Eric. "Feel like watching some TV, or would you rather do something else?"

Eric stood and pressed himself against Zac. "What I'd really like is a nice hot bath." He ran his index finger between Zac's pecs to land on the fly of his zipper. "Feel like joining me?"

Just like that, Zac's cock hardened. "Try to keep me away," he teased, pulling Eric towards the bathroom.

"The tubs not that big, but I'm sure we can both squeeze in."

Zac shut the bathroom door to keep the heat in and turned on the faucet. Once the water warmed up, he put the plug in and reached for Eric. He pulled Eric's shirt over his head, noticing how thin and frail his body appeared. Zac ran his hand over the slightly concave stomach, liking the feel of soft skin beneath his fingers. "You should take better care of yourself. You're too thin."

Before he knew what was happening, Eric had pushed him away and picked his shirt up from the floor. "Fuck it," Eric spat, opening the bathroom door.

"Hey. Hey!" Zac shouted, reaching for Eric. "What the hell's going on?"

Eric spun around with fire in his eyes. "You jocks are all the same. I'll never be strong enough, big enough for you. I'm who I am. If I couldn't change for my father, I sure as hell can't change for you."

"Whoa, whoa, I didn't mean it like that." Zac put his hands on Eric's shoulders. "I'm sorry if I pissed you off." When Eric didn't move away, Zac pulled the smaller man against his chest. "I don't know about the other men you've been with, and don't even get me started on your dad, but I think you're the sexiest man I've ever known." Zac ran his hands down Eric's back. "I said what I did because I'm worried you aren't taking care of yourself, that's all. I want you to be healthy. I can tell you're naturally small, but I can also tell you're thinner than you should be."

Eric rubbed his face against Zac's chest. "I don't gross you out?"

Zac thrust his cock against Eric's stomach. "Does that answer your question?"

Lifting the bottom of Zac's shirt, Eric kissed his way up the pleasure trail to Zac's nipple. A warm tongue flicked over the pebbled nub, eliciting a groan from Zac. "The tub's going to overflow before we even get in," he mumbled, holding the back of Eric's head in place.

Eric gave Zac's nipple a gentle nip before releasing it. "Can't have that," he declared with a grin.

Zac reluctantly pulled away and shut off the water. He took off his shirt and let some of the water out while he kicked out of his shoes. Not waiting for Eric, Zac stripped out of the rest of his clothes and climbed into the tub. "Ooh, yeah, that's nice," he groaned, sinking as far down as he could.

Gazing up at a naked Eric, Zac held out his hand. "Told you it would be a tight fit."

Eric climbed in, putting the bulk of his body down at the end of the tub between Zac's feet. "Now that doesn't look comfortable," Zac said, gesturing for Eric to come closer.

With an impish grin, Eric kissed his way up Zac's torso to his lips. With Eric lying on top of Zac, the majority of his small body was out of the water.

Eric must've realised it because he chuckled. "My ass is gonna get cold."

Zac splashed some of the hot water over Eric's tight buns before covering them with his hands. "Can't have that, can we?" He could feel Eric's erection press against his abdomen and there was no doubt Eric could feel his cock.

Eric rubbed his soft lips over every square inch of Zac's face before connecting with his mouth once again. Zac opened to the questing tongue as he ran his fingers down the crack of Eric's ass. Damn, why hadn't he thought to grab a condom?

Eric moaned and moved his legs up as much as he could, giving Zac more room to play. "That's nice."

Zac reached for the bar of soap and slicked his hands, before slowly inserting a finger deep into Eric's ass. "I wanna make love to you," Zac whispered. When his fingers moved in and out of Eric's passage easily, he added another. "Would you like that? My cock where my fingers are?"

"Yesss," Eric hissed, riding Zac's hand.

"Can you make it to the bedroom?" Zac removed his fingers and massaged the cheeks of Eric's ass.

Without another word, Eric stood and climbed from the tub. Zac watched as his lover began to dry off. When Eric gave him another one of those grins and bent over to dry his feet, Zac pounced. He put his hands on Eric's slim hips and drew him back towards the tub. Separating Eric's cheeks, Zac ran his tongue over the stretched hole. The hint of soap didn't deter him in the least, he delved his tongue inside as far as it would go.

Eric's knees started to buckle and Zac pulled back. "Easy. Wouldn't want you to hurt yourself." He steadied his lover and climbed out of the tub. Eric turned and began drying the water from Zac's skin. Damn, it was nice to have someone take care of him. He hadn't realised how much he missed having a lover do the small things that lovers do for each other.

Eric tossed the towel over his shoulder and took Zac's hand. "Lead on."

With a lecherous grin plastered to his face, Zac walked them both to his bedroom. He tossed the covers to the end of the bed and pulled the needed supplies out of the bedside drawer.

He could see the nervous energy running through Eric by the way the smaller man shifted from foot to foot. Zac wondered how long it had been since Eric had been with a man. Although it wouldn't be polite to ask, Zac decided to go easy on him and make the first move. He crawled onto the centre of the bed, spread his thighs and opened his arms in invitation.

Eric appeared to release a breath he'd been holding and crawled into Zac's arms. "Nervous?" Zac asked, running his fingers through Eric's messy curls.

"Is it that obvious?" Eric chuckled.

Zac rolled them until Eric lay underneath him. He braced his much heavier weight on his arms and looked down at the incredibly sexy man. "I'll go slow," he promised.

Eric shook his head. "I don't want you to. That's part of the problem."

"Why is that a problem?" If Eric wanted to be fucked shamelessly into the mattress, Zac knew he was more than up to the task.

"Because I've never wanted anyone the way I want you." Eric stared towards the window. "I don't want to need you."

Zac curled his body around Eric's and reached for the lube. "What's wrong with needing someone? I'd like to know, because I seem to need you lately like I need my next breath." As he talked, Zac poured a large dollop of lube onto his fingers.

He watched Eric's eyes droop as he circled his lover's hole before pushing inside.

"I'm not a good relationship risk," Eric finally told him, as Zac introduced another finger.

Rimming Eric's lips with his tongue, he delved in for a kiss. Pulling back, he gazed into Eric's eyes. "I guess it all depends on why you're not a good risk. Is it because you're not interested in a relationship, or because you don't feel you have the time?"

Eric moved his hips, fucking himself on Zac's hand like he'd done earlier. "Time," he gasped.

Zac could tell Eric was ready for him. He removed his fingers and tore open the foil packet, using his teeth to aid him. Once sheathed, Zac momentarily put their conversation aside to make love to the man under him. He slid his cock in, relishing in the tight heat of Eric's channel. "Damn," Zac groaned.

Fully seated, he waited for Eric's body to accommodate his length and girth. Eric opened his eyes and grabbed the back of Zac's head, pulling him down for a kiss. The tongue thrusting into his mouth, so erotic, Zac was on edge in no time. He began to move his hips, pulling out before plunging back inside.

Eric broke the kiss and looked pleadingly at Zac. "Okay, baby, I know what you need." Zac hooked his arms under Eric's knees and spread his lover as much as he dared. Picking up speed, the sound of flesh smacking flesh was overwhelmingly loud in the small bedroom.

Their fucking may not have lasted as long as Zac had hoped, but they had plenty of time to correct that. His orgasm blind-sided him when Eric reached between them to squeeze and twist his nipples.

"Fuuuck!" Zac howled, emptying his load into the condom.

Eric released one of Zac's nipples to wrap his hand around his cock. It only took Eric four good strokes to shoot string after string of seed between them. Eric released his cock seconds before Zac's arms gave out.

Zac collapsed to the side, releasing Eric's legs as he did. His breathing was completely out of control as his body continued to quake from the intense climax. He opened his eyes to gaze at Eric and found his lover seemed to be having the same problem. Zac lifted a hand to Eric's chest and rubbed the hairless skin in small circles.

Once he could speak without passing out, Zac hummed. "I could get used to that."

"Yeah," Eric answered, covering Zac's hand with his own.

They lay in that position for several moments before Zac licked his lips. He'd never in his life asked a lover to live with him. In this case though, not only did he really want Eric in his bed every night, but it seemed like a sensible solution to the time problem. "You know, if you moved in here, you could quit your job at Poppie's."

Eric turned to his side and stared at Zac. "I can't. My job is the only thing putting food in my stomach and gas in my car."

From the looks of it, not much of Eric's money went towards food, but Zac wasn't about to say that out loud. "Didn't you say you had six months left before you'd start getting paid by the hospital?"

"Yeah."

He could tell by the expression on Eric's face, his lover was too proud to live completely off the money Zac made. He quickly came up with a compromise. "If you cut back your hours at Poppie's to a couple days a week, you should make more than enough to pay for gas. The rest I can handle for six months without any hardship."

"We've only known each other for two weeks," Eric said.

"I know, but I also know what I want and that's to spend more time with you." *Shit.* "Unless of course you don't want that?" he added, suddenly insecure.

Eric moulded his body against Zac's. "I do." He placed a kiss on Zac's chest. "I'll give it some thought, okay?"

"Sure," Zac answered, kissing the top of Eric's head. "I couldn't ask for any more than that."

Within minutes, Eric was asleep. Zac laid there thinking about the whirlwind relationship that had blossomed between the two of them. Although he was afraid of getting hurt, he'd never been with anyone he felt like fighting for, until Eric. *Hell, what if I have to fight Eric for Eric?*

Glancing at the clock, he saw the time was quickly approaching for Eric to report to his job at Poppie's. He looked at the sleeping man pressed to his side. *This is what he needs.* Zac carefully climbed out of bed without waking his lover. Knowing it might get him into hot water, Zac put in a call to Eric's uncle.

Chapter Six

The sound of crying woke Zac. He rolled over and realised it was Eric. Sometime during the night his lover had pulled away from Zac and was now rolled into a ball on the edge of the bed.

Zac scooted over far enough to reach for Eric and pulled him against his chest. He knew why the smaller man was crying, so he didn't ask. Zac simply held onto the man he was seriously falling for.

"It's okay," Zac soothed, kissing the top of Eric's head. "Just hold on to me and we'll get through it."

Eric continued to cry. "She had blue eyes," he stuttered around the tears.

Zac felt his own eyes begin to sting as tears threatened. He had always had the utmost respect for nurses and doctors, but never more so than at that moment. Sure, he knew it must be hard to see people die day in and day out, but he'd never witnessed the effects first hand, until now.

He wished there was something he could say to make Eric feel better, but Zac wasn't a psychologist. What if he said the wrong thing and it only made Eric feel worse? He decided maybe just listening was the best thing to do. "I'm here if you need to talk," he whispered, holding Eric tighter.

Eric shook his head. "I can't get her face out of my head. Her eyes. They only opened once, but they seemed to plead with me to save her, to make the pain stop." Eric gasped as another sob hit him. "And I couldn't."

Eric wiped at the tears dripping onto Zac's chest. "I know I can't save everyone, but I wanted to save *her*," Eric hiccupped.

Zac found the top corner of the sheet and wiped Eric's face, including his nose. Sheets could easily be washed, but listening to his lover cry was breaking his heart. Eric had been asleep for almost eight hours. Zac began to wonder if Dr. Peters had been wrong. What if Eric's breakdown wasn't due in part to fatigue? What if his lover really couldn't handle the deaths that were a part of his line of work?

Eric's sobs began to die down. "Thanks," Eric mumbled.

Zac ran a comforting hand down Eric's bony spine. "I've got ya, and I've no plans to let you go."

Eventually Eric drifted off to sleep, with a sniffle only now and then. Zac tried to go back to sleep. He knew he needed to talk to someone about how to support his lover in his time of need. Maybe Angelo knew someone? Zac made a mental note to call his friend in the morning.

* * * *

"Eric? I'm leaving," Zac's voice filtered through his dreams.

Rolling over, Eric opened his sore and swollen eyes. Zac's gorgeous face loomed over his. "Hey," he greeted without trying to breathe out. When Zac didn't immediately back off, Eric turned his head and took some much needed oxygen into his lungs.

Zac chuckled. "Morning breath?"

"Yep."

Zac held up a glass of orange juice. "Here, drink this. It'll mask the breath so I can get my kiss before I leave." Zac handed Eric the juice and stood.

Leaning up on an elbow, Eric drank his breakfast as he watched his lover move around the room. "I can't believe it's morning already," Eric groaned. "Shit!"

Zac rushed back over to the bed. "What's wrong?" he asked, looking concerned.

"I didn't go to work. Uncle Lewis is gonna kill me." Damn, how could he have fallen asleep? He knew better than to try and catch cat naps in between his jobs.

Zac leaned over and kissed Eric's shoulder. "Relax. After you fell asleep I called Lewis. He's a nice guy. I'm glad I'm not the only one who worries about the kind of hours you put in. Anyway, he said to tell you if you needed a couple days off just to let him know so he could call in his backup guy."

A couple of days off. What did that feel like? It had been over eighteen months since he'd had a full day off. He'd have to sit down later and go over his cheque book. Maybe he'd take the entire weekend and start back on his normal routine on Monday. Eric felt almost giddy thinking about an entire weekend with Zac.

"We'll see," he finally agreed. "I need to check a few things. I've got to pay my car insurance at the end of the month." He finished off the juice and set the glass on the table. He could see the urge to offer financial assistance in Zac's expression.

Eric tapped his lips. "You can kiss me now."

Zac lay down next to him and pulled him into his arms. "You know, I…"

Eric shut Zac up with a kiss. He wouldn't take his lover's money, not when he was perfectly capable of earning it himself. He moaned when Zac's hand slid from his hip to his ass. Eric wanted to be fucked again, but he knew Zac was already late for work. He sighed and broke the kiss. "You'd better get going."

"You know, if you stay in bed until I come home for lunch, I could probably get someone to cover for me for an extended break."

Eric moaned. The thought of Zac's cock buried deep in his ass was somehow comforting. "Deal."

Zac gave him one last kiss, sweeping the interior of Eric's mouth with his tongue. Breaking away, Zac stood and gazed down at him. "Would it freak you out if I told you I was falling in love with you?"

It should, Eric knew, but it didn't. Maybe that was telling of his own feelings towards the man standing over him. "Actually, it gives me peace."

Zac's smile lit up his entire face. He took one last quick kiss. "I might be home early for lunch," Zac said with a wink.

After Zac left, Eric threw off the covers and stumbled into the bathroom. The room still smelled of Zac's cologne. Eric inhaled deeply as he relieved himself. He looked at the shower, but decided to take one later. What he really wanted was to go back to sleep. Damn. One day off and he was already becoming a layabout.

Walking back into the bedroom, he shut the heavy window curtains and shrouded the room in darkness. *Fantastic. I need some of those curtains.*

He snuggled under the blankets and buried his face in Zac's pillow. He fell asleep with Zac's smell comforting him.

* * * *

Zac set the last of the grocery sacks on the counter. After dropping Eric off at his car, Zac had stopped by the store to stock up on food. He got junky stuff for the poker game, and healthy foods he could prepare for Eric.

Zac glanced at the clock when his doorbell rang. It was too early for the guys to show up, and Eric said he was going by his place to get more of his clothes. After he'd returned home from another victorious football game, Zac had somehow managed to convince Eric to stay at least a few more days.

The doorbell rang again, disrupting his thoughts on the hours of lovemaking the two of them had enjoyed. Zac sauntered towards the door, positive he knew exactly who it was. He opened to Marco's dirty but smiling face.

"Did your water get shut off or what?" he asked, letting Marco inside.

"No, thank you very much. I pay my bills. It's just that rat bastard I used to call a friend still has me working out in Bumfuck, Egypt." Marco barely slowed before heading into the bathroom.

"Remember what I told you last time," Zac reminded him.

"Yeah, yeah. I'll clean the tub when I'm done," Marco answered, shutting the door.

Zac shook his head and went back into the kitchen to finish putting away the groceries. He felt much better after his earlier call to Dr. Sidney Brennon, a psychiatrist friend of Angelo's. According to Sid, as he asked to be called, Eric needed the space to work things out on his own with a strong support system to back him up when needed. Zac knew supporting Eric wouldn't be a hardship in any way. The more he was around his lover, the deeper he fell.

He left the sacks of junk food on the counter and had just started getting out the table leaf and extra chairs when the doorbell rang again. Zac propped the leaf against the wall and went to answer it. By the time he got to the living room, Marco was also headed for the door, his waist wrapped in a towel. "Go put some clothes on," he admonished, opening the door.

He turned his head to greet his guest and saw the wide-eyed stare of his lover. Eric's eyes swung from a half-nude Marco and back to him. "Sorry, bad timing," Eric mumbled and turned to leave.

"Wait!" Zac followed Eric as he ran down the stairs. He finally managed to get a hand on the smaller man's arms once he'd reached the bottom. "Eric, stop!" He turned Eric to face him.

Zac could tell by the sheen in Eric's eyes his lover was about to cry again. "That's Marco," he tried to explain.

"I don't give a shit what his name is," Eric spat.

Zac took a deep breath, trying to calm his racing heart. "He's one of the guys I play poker with. He just came from work and was filthy and asked to take a shower." He gave Eric a gentle shake. "I am not sleeping with him, nor have I ever."

Eric stared up at him for several seconds before his chin lowered to his chest. "Sorry. Guess I just made an ass out of myself in front of your friend."

Zac pulled Eric into his arms. "I couldn't give a shit about what Marco thinks. The only thing that matters to me right now is what you think." He tilted Eric's chin up for a kiss. "Come inside?"

Eric nodded and picked up the duffle that had flown out of his hand when Zac grabbed him. Zac took the bag and led Eric back up the steps. As soon as they stepped into the apartment, they were once again greeted by Marco, only this time he actually had on a pair of Zac's sweats and a T-shirt.

"Sorry," Eric apologised.

Marco chuckled and shook his head. "If I saw a half-naked man standing in the middle of my lover's living room, I'd probably react the same way."

A snort came from the doorway. Zac glanced over his shoulder to see Kent standing there.

"Hell, you'd probably just ask to join them," Kent accused, staring at Marco.

"Fuck off," Marco spat and walked into the kitchen.

Carol Lynne

"Eric, I'd like you to meet Kent Baker," Zac introduced.

"Nice to finally meet you," Kent greeted, shaking Eric's hand. "You plan on sticking around to play with us?"

Eric looked up at Zac. "Uh, I thought I'd stick around, but I don't know how to play poker."

"Hell, if Marco can learn to play anyone can," Kent chuckled.

"I heard that!" Marco yelled from the kitchen, reappearing with a bag of chips in his hands.

Kent grinned. "Seriously, I don't think any of us mind showing you the ropes if you want to play."

"Thanks. I think I just might," Eric answered.

Zac held up Eric's duffle. "I'm gonna go toss this into the bedroom." He didn't miss the questioning glances his friends threw his way. Let them think what they wanted. Eric in his bed every night was worth the razzing he was most likely to get.

While he was at it, Zac opened the bottom dresser drawer he'd cleared out earlier and put Eric's clothes away. He hoped it would make Eric feel more welcomed. By the time he walked back into the living room, Angelo and Trey had joined them. "So we're just missing Bobby?"

"Yeah," Trey agreed. "I talked to him earlier and he said he had an afternoon cruise along the shoreline, but he should be here in time. If not, to start without him."

"Cool. Well why don't we go ahead and play a couple of practice rounds so Eric can get a feel for the game." *Shit.* He hadn't thought of the money aspect. He looked at his friends. "We are playing for change

75

again, *right*?" He said it in such a way that his friends should catch his meaning.

"Yeah, of course." Kent gave Zac a wink. "Shoot, I forgot to get more beer," Kent proclaimed. "I'm gonna run to the store, does anyone need anything?"

Most of the guys pulled bills out of their pockets. "Yeah, could you pick me up some change?" Angelo asked.

"Sure." Kent collected money from everyone except Eric.

Eric shot Zac a nervous glance. Walking over, Zac took Eric's hand and pulled him into the kitchen. "Don't worry. I've got a big change bowl on the dresser. We can both dip into it."

Eric reached up and pulled Zac's head down for a kiss. "Thanks, but I'm not stupid. I can tell you guys don't normally play for change."

Zac grinned. "Won't hurt them. Maybe it'll loosen 'em up a bit."

* * * *

Eric studied the cards in his hands. They weren't bad, but they weren't really good either. "Fold," he announced, tossing the cards face down on the table. He might've taken the chance if he was playing with his own money, but he'd already managed to lose close to twelve dollars.

He finished his beer and stood to get another. "Anyone?"

"Sure, I could use another," Bobby said.

Eric ran his fingers through the hairs on Zac's nape. "What about you? Can I get you something?"

Zac removed Eric's hand from the back of his neck and kissed it. "No thanks, I'm good, love."

Eric couldn't miss the snickers when he turned his back. "Shut up," Zac reprimanded them.

He started to reach for a beer, but thought better of it. He'd already had his limit. Any more and he was most likely to get emotional again. It seemed to be a constant battle to keep the tears at bay. The breakdown a couple nights ago still weighed heavily on his mind. It wasn't like him to cry in the first place, but especially not where someone could see him.

The fact that Zac hadn't judged him, told Eric more than words ever could. He pulled a beer out of the sink and handed it to Bobby. "Thanks." Bobby smiled.

"No problem." He went back into the kitchen and retrieved a glass out of the cupboard. He fixed himself a nice glass of ice water and once again took his seat next to Zac. As soon as he was seated, his hand found its way to Zac's thigh.

Zac glanced at him with a grin. "You're not trying to ruin my concentration, are you?"

Eric moved his hand up Zac's thigh to gently squeeze his lover's cock through his sweats. "Now, if I were trying to ruin your game, I'd be doing this," Eric teased.

Zac leaned over and kissed him. "I might not mind losing a hand or two if you're going to keep that up."

"Hey, hey, hey," Kent admonished them. "It's not fair that Eric gets a squeeze toy and we don't," the big man joked.

"I've got all the toy you could ask for," Marco declared, looking straight at Kent.

Kent cleared his throat and grumbled. "Not interested in hand-me-downs."

What started as a teasing exchange soon turned ugly. Marco jumped up and threw his hand of cards in Kent's face. "Fuck you, old man."

Kent narrowed his eyes and stood. "Like I said, I'm not interested in hand-me-downs."

Eric jumped as Marco hurled himself over Trey to grab Kent's shirt. "I may be a flirt, but I'm not a fucking slut, and I'm sick of your constant innuendos."

Kent didn't move. He simply stared right back at Marco. "If you want to keep those hands, I suggest you get them off of me. Now."

Zac and Bobby both stood and separated the two arguing friends. Eric didn't know what to do. He suddenly felt like an outsider. After all, he really didn't know any of the men except Zac, and the way Kent and Marco were squaring off, Eric knew there had to be a story there.

"Enough!" Zac screamed when Marco started to say something back to Kent.

Marco eventually released his hold on Kent's shirt and stepped back. He scooped his winnings from the table and put them into his pocket. "I'll catch you guys later," he sighed and walked out of the room.

Zac turned his attention to Kent. "You gonna calm down and play?"

Kent dropped to his chair. "I think I'll sit this game out."

Zac walked back around the table and resumed the game. "You need to deal with that," Zac mumbled.

"Mind your own business," Kent mumbled back.

"I will as long as it doesn't carry over into my house," Zac answered, tossing a chip into the pot.

Chapter Seven

"I think I need to go back to work," Eric announced, putting the book he'd been reading on the coffee table.

Zac reached for the remote and turned down the football game he'd been watching. "You sure? Dr. Peters thought maybe it would be a good idea for you to talk to one of the grief counsellors."

Eric rolled to his back and looked up at Zac. "I don't think I need counselling. It's not every death that affects me. It was just something about that particular little girl. I've mourned, now it's time to get back to life."

Zac brushed the wayward curls out of Eric's eyes. He hated the thought of not spending time together the way they had for the previous several days. Even this, just sitting on the couch together with Eric's head in his lap was nice. He tried to think of what was best for Eric and not himself. "What about the delivery job? Have you come to a decision on that?"

Eric's cheeks flushed. "Uh, yeah. I think I need to keep the job for a while at least. I know it means spending less time together, but I need the money. And before you say anything, yes, I'm still considering your offer. Maybe if things continue to work out between us, I can cut back on my hours at Poppie's, but for now, I've got bills that need to be paid."

"So I'm back to seeing you one night a week for a couple hours? Believe me, Eric, it's worth it to me to pay your car insurance to spend time with you."

Eric reached up and rubbed Zac's chest through his T-shirt. "I told you I was still thinking about your offer, that's all I can give you at the moment."

Zac started to get pissed. He knew he was being selfish, but dammit, he didn't want to go back to the way things were before. "Hell, I'll spend more on pizzas than you'll even make in tips for the week. It doesn't make sense to me."

Eric sat up and put his feet on the floor. "And it doesn't make sense to me why a man I've only known a few weeks would offer to give me money in exchange for living with him." Eric rose and walked into the bathroom, shutting the door with a bang.

"Fuck!" He thought he meant more to Eric than that. Zac mimicked Eric's earlier statement exaggerating the hand motions. "Well fine. Forget I asked!" he yelled loud enough for Eric to hear him.

He grabbed his keys from the table and walked out the door. Zac knew he'd be coming home to an empty apartment, but he didn't feel like being there when Eric left. He climbed into his jeep and headed towards the marina.

* * * *

Eric flinched when the front door slammed. He gazed at himself in the mirror. "Well, that's one way to fuck up a relationship." He shook his head. Why had he ever thought it would work out?

He started going through the hamper and pulled out some of his dirty clothes. Sadly, they looked right at home mixed in with Zac's. Pulling out one of Zac's shirts, Eric held it to his face. He wondered if Zac would miss it if it mysteriously found its way into his duffle.

Clutching the shirt to his chest, Eric went into the bedroom and began packing his things. He should've known when he'd discovered Zac had cleared out a drawer for him that the man was a control freak. It wasn't that Eric wouldn't have eventually taken Zac up on his offer to help out, but he thought they needed a little more time to be sure. Why was that so wrong?

Yeah, he was falling head over heels for the guy, but that didn't mean he could drop everything he'd worked so hard for. Why didn't Zac see that? Six more months of working two jobs and he'd be free to quit working for his uncle.

In the end Eric figured it was better this way. A doctor's job wasn't strictly a nine to five occupation. If Zac couldn't deal with Eric's work schedule it would eventually turn into a huge source of resentment on both sides.

Eric used the spare set of keys Zac had given him to lock up the apartment. He put the key under the welcome mat and headed back to his old life.

* * * *

"You're up," Kent reminded him, gesturing to the pot.

"Oh, sorry." Zac tossed in a chip, mindless of the cards in his hands. He felt like he was living on empty. Even taking his football team to the state championship game hadn't lifted his spirits. The fact that they'd lost was beside the point. He'd even blown his family off at Thanksgiving and stayed in California, hoping against hope that Eric would call or come by.

"You playing or what?" Bobby asked.

Zac glanced around the table. "Sorry, where are we at?"

Bobby gave him a sympathetic smile. "It's just you and me. You want to raise or call?"

Zac studied at his cards, horrified to find he had an absolutely shitty hand. What the hell had he been thinking betting money against this crap pile? "Fold." He tossed his cards onto the table and stretched.

"Haven't heard from Eric, huh?" Bobby asked.

"No. I'm sure he's back working twenty-hour days again. Probably isn't even eating right." It had been over a month since the stupid argument. Zac tried leaving a couple of messages on Eric's phone, but they went unanswered.

"I should just forget about him," Zac sighed.

"But you can't," Kent added to the conversation.

"No." He wasn't used to talking to his buddies about relationship stuff, and it was starting to feel a little awkward. Zac picked up his beer and finished it in one gulp. "Anyone need another?"

"Yeah, grab me one. I'm gonna hit the head," Kent announced and as he walked along the hall and into the bathroom.

Zac opened another beer for himself and set one on the table for Kent. "Okay, time to get my head back into the game," Zac said, clapping his hands before rubbing them for luck.

Forty minutes later the doorbell rang. Zac looked up from his cards to see Kent's face had turned bright red. "What did you do?" he asked his friend.

"Nothin'. Just got hungry so I thought I'd order us something to eat."

Zac's brow rose as he gestured to the food he'd prepared on the counter. "Something wrong with sloppy Joes?"

"Just wanted pizza is all." Kent started to stand, but Zac stood first.

"I'll get it. No telling what you'd say to Eric. Probably make me out to be a love-sick fool," he mumbled on the way through the living room.

When he opened the door he was shocked to see a stranger standing on his deck holding a pizza. "Where's Eric?"

The kid looked at him like he was crazy. "Eric quit right after the mugging."

Zac's heart almost burst out of his chest. "What? He was mugged?"

"Yeah, 'bout three weeks ago delivering to an apartment. Some guys jumped him getting into the elevator." The kid shrugged like it was no big deal. "That'll be fifteen forty-seven."

Zac quickly pulled a twenty out of his pocket and gave it to the kid. "Thanks." He shut the door and hurried to the kitchen, tossing the pizza in the centre of the table. "Gotta go. The delivery guy told me Eric was mugged a couple of weeks ago and hasn't worked since." Zac quickly cashed in his chips and pocketed his meagre winnings.

"Keep on playing if you want," Zac said, going to the kitchen to make up a goody-bag for Eric. If Eric hadn't been working, that most likely meant he hadn't been eating either. *Dammit, why didn't he call me?*

By the time Zac arrived at Eric's door, he was filled with mixed emotions. He pounded on the door a little harder than he probably should have, but eventually Eric opened.

"Zac? What're you doing here?"

"Can I come in?" Zac studied Eric's face looking for any signs of the mugging.

Eric eventually stepped back and gestured towards the interior of his apartment. "Sorry it's such a mess. I wasn't expecting company."

Eric shut the door and walked over to the futon that appeared to be used as both a couch and a bed. It was presently unfolded into a bed. Eric pulled the cover off and slid it back into a sofa.

The entire time Eric worked, Zac couldn't take his eyes off the man he loved. Eric's spine was even more prominent than usual. Zac guessed his lover had lost at least ten pounds in the last month. Ten pounds that Eric's already-thin frame couldn't afford.

"I brought some sloppy Joes with me," Zac announced, holding up the paper sack. "I made them for the guys, but they didn't seem interested," he rambled on.

Eric gestured to the couch and sat down. "Thanks, but I'm not hungry."

"The hell you're not." Zac joined Eric on the uncomfortable sofa.

"Please don't start," Eric sighed.

As much as Zac wanted to ask about the mugging, he could tell Eric was already on the defensive. "So, how're things at the hospital?"

"The same. Four months and three weeks to go. Dr. Peters did offer me a resident position though, so that's good."

"Are you kidding? That's great." Zac had secretly been worried that Eric would have to move out of the area.

"Yeah," Eric responded in a noncommittal fashion.

They sat in silence for a few moments, both of them apparently at a loss as to what to say. "I miss you," Zac finally blurted.

"I miss you, too," Eric mumbled.

"Can I ask why you didn't return my calls?"

Eric stood and walked towards the window. "Since I'm pretty sure the reason you're here is because you heard what happened, it seems I was right not to call."

"What's that supposed to mean?" Zac asked with a combination of confusion and anger.

"I was still pretty upset for a week or so, then I got mugged, and I had a lot of time to think, but I couldn't call you at that point."

"Why not?"

Eric shrugged. "I was afraid you'd think the only reason I was calling was because I wasn't working. I didn't want you to feel sorry for me and come to my rescue." Eric pointed to the sack on the floor at Zac's feet. "Bringing me food and stuff because you knew I couldn't afford groceries."

There was a moment in which Zac actually questioned his motives. Had he rushed over in hopes of rescuing Eric? The more he thought about it, the more resolved he became. "No. To be honest, I guess I used what happened as an excuse to see you. It doesn't matter what I do, I can't stop missing you. I even stayed home over Thanksgiving in hopes that you'd call."

Eric turned away from the window and walked towards Zac. "I worked on Thanksgiving, but I thought of you, too."

Taking a chance, Zac stood and held out his arms. The corner of Eric's mouth tipped up as he walked into Zac's embrace. Zac lifted the smaller man off the ground and kissed him, putting all the love he felt into that one action.

Breaking for air, Zac set Eric's feet back on the floor. "Come home with me," he whispered against Eric's lips.

"I have to work in the morning."

Zac rimmed Eric's lips with his tongue. "I'll set the alarm." He tilted Eric's chin up and gazed into his eyes. "Please. Even if we do nothing but hold each other."

Eric bit his lip and glanced around the room. "Yeah, I'd like that," he finally said. "Hang on, let me get my clothes."

Zac watched as Eric started going through a pile of dirty clothes. He picked up a pair of dark blue cotton pants and looked at them before draping them over his arm.

"What're you doing?" Zac couldn't help asking.

Eric grinned. "Been a while since I've been able to do laundry. Just trying to find a not-so-dirty pair of pants."

Zac chuckled. "At college I lived out of the dirty clothes pile. When I moved down here and got the apartment, I almost kissed the landlord when he told me it came with a washer and dryer."

"Yeah," Eric laughed. "You never really think about how your clothes get clean when you're growing up."

"Will you get pissed if I tell you to bag up your clothes and wash 'em at my place?"

Eric seemed to study him for a few seconds before smiling. "I could do that. Thanks."

"Well, you know, I wouldn't want your patients to smell you coming before you got there."

"They're not that bad." Eric glanced down at the clothes in his hand. "On second thoughts, yeah, maybe they are."

* * * *

Eric took the soap off the shelf and poured a capful into the running water. A warm naked body pressed against his back as lips began to tease his neck. Eric shut the washing machine lid and tilted his neck to the side.

Zac broke his hold on Eric's neck only long enough to pull his T-shirt over his head. "I've missed the feel of your body against mine," Zac admitted.

"Mmm," Eric moaned as Zac began unfastening his pants.

"Good thinking. I should probably wash these at the same time." Eric bent over to untie his shoes and Zac pressed against his ass. "Now you're just teasing me," Eric chuckled.

"No teasing about it. I want you." Zac waited for Eric to get his pants into the washer before spinning him around. "Now." He picked Eric up and set him on top of the washer.

It was then that Eric noticed the bottle of lube and condom sitting on the dryer. "In here?" he questioned.

Zac nodded his head. "You ever fuck through the spin cycle?"

Eric laughed and spread his legs to accommodate Zac. He wrapped his legs around the bigger man and pulled him ever closer. "Can't say as I have," he said, running his tongue around Zac's pebbled nipple.

"Truthfully, neither have I, but it's always been a fantasy."

Zac hissed when Eric took the sensitive bud of flesh between his teeth and bit down gently. "You like that?" he asked.

"What do you think?" Zac reached for the tube of lube and poured some onto his fingers.

Eric brought his legs up to rest his heels on the edge of the washer. As tall as Zac was, Eric still didn't quite understand mechanically how they could do this. Zac's cock was even with the top edge of the washer, but he'd have to stand on tip-toes to reach and even then it just didn't seem possible. "I think you need something to stand on."

Zac looked down, his brows drawing together. "Well, shit."

Eric started to giggle. "Reality isn't always as good as the fantasy."

"Speak for yourself." Zac disappeared into the kitchen before returning with a plastic step-stool.

Eric's giggle turned into a laugh. "No. I can't let you stand on that thing. You're gonna fall, crack your head open and then I'll have to stitch you up."

"Leave it to the master," Zac announced, stepping up onto the stool. "Perfect." He looked at his once lubed fingers. "Where the hell did it go?"

Eric held his stomach. It had been ages since he'd laughed so hard and never had he done it while naked. He watched Zac roll the condom on and pour more lube onto his fingers. The moment one of those long digits was up close and personal with Eric's hole, all laughter stopped.

He reached between his legs and gave his sac a squeeze, making sure to stare Zac in the eyes as he did it.

"You're a sexy little fucker, you know that?" Zac asked, adding another finger.

Eric shook his head. He had a mirror. The weight-loss had erased anything sexy about him. But when Zac looked at him like he was doing just then, Eric felt sexy. "Fuck me," he whispered, sliding his hand up to fist his own cock.

Zac's nostrils flared. He removed his fingers and replaced them with the head of his cock. "It's been a while, so let me know if I'm going too fast."

Eric smiled. Even in a state of extreme sexual need, Zac's feelings still came through. He nodded his head in acknowledgement and sighed as the crown of Zac's cock eased past his outer ring of muscles.

The expression on Zac's face was a cross between concentration and need. He could tell Zac wanted to push in to the hilt but held himself back. Yeah, that's the look he'd fallen in love with. Since they'd met, Zac had always put Eric's needs before his own.

"Please," Eric begged. He wanted to see that expression change to one of total bliss.

Zac rocked his hips back and forth until he was buried completely in Eric's ass. Eric watched the muscles in Zac's jaws flex as his lover ground his teeth. "I'm not made of glass," he reminded Zac.

With a relieved sigh, Zac began to move. As Eric's body adjusted to the invasion, Zac fucked him harder. Eric could feel the edge of the washer digging into the top of his ass as he moved his legs to rest over Zac's broad shoulders.

Zac started to slow his pace and Eric opened his eyes. "What's wrong?"

"I'm waiting for the washer to catch up."

"Huh?" Eric was on the edge of ecstasy and Zac was worried about the damn laundry?

"Spin-cycle's coming up," Zac grunted.

Oh, the fantasy. "Okay, but I'm not waiting. Spin-cycle be dammed." Eric continued jacking his cock, as Zac maintained a steady rhythm in and out of his ass. The feelings were too intense to wait on the stupid washing machine.

The second the spin-cycle started, Eric changed his mind. "Oh, fuck!" he screamed. The cum erupted from his cock to land on his stomach in long ropes.

Zac grunted, increasing the intensity of his thrust as Eric's body vibrated with the machine under him. Oh, God, Eric took back every laugh or giggle. Zac's fantasy totally rocked.

Zac howled Eric's name as he slammed inside once more. Eric watched Zac's body jerk as he emptied his seed deep into the condom. Suddenly, Zac dropped, his cock pulling free of Eric's ass. Eric lost his balance on the edge of the washer and began to fall with Zac.

Strong arms caught him before he reached the floor. Stunned, Eric looked around. "What happened?"

Zac started laughing and pointed towards the stool. "I guess I exceeded the weight limit."

Eric glanced down and started laughing at the flattened plastic step. Zac held Eric in his arms and they continued to laugh together. "You're gonna have to get a sturdier stool because we *have* to do that again."

Chapter Eight

The alarm went off precisely at four-thirty. Zac reached over and hit the snooze button. He kissed Eric's shoulder and snuggled once again to his back. As much as he wanted to not wake the sleeping man in his arms, he knew it had to be done. If Eric didn't get to work on time when he stayed the night, he would be very reluctant to stay over in the future, and Zac wanted his lover there every night.

"Eric? It's four-thirty." Zac ran his hand down Eric's side. "Are you awake?"

"I don't wanna get up," Eric whined and turned over to face Zac.

"Then we're in agreement, but we both know you have to." Zac grinned, helping brush the crusty stuff away from Eric's eyes. He'd stayed awake long after Eric had drifted off to sleep. He needed to know about the mugging. It was killing him not knowing.

"Did they catch the guys who jumped you?" he finally asked. He felt Eric stiffen in his arms.

"No. They wore ski masks. The police think it had been planned in advance. When they went to question the person who phoned in the pizza, it was an old woman. She said she didn't order anything." Eric shrugged. "Guess they used her address to get me into the building."

"Did they...hurt you?" Dozens of scenarios had gone through his mind since he'd heard of the attack.

"Not really. There were three of 'em. Needless to say, I didn't offer much resistance. They did all that and walked away with less than a hundred bucks."

"What'll you do now?" Zac asked. "Because you know my previous offer still stands."

Eric rolled onto his back and rubbed his eyes. "I think I quit delivering more because I was tired and it reminded me too much of you. There's no reason I shouldn't just get another job. I sold blood last week to pick up a couple bucks."

Zac was horrified. Not that there was anything wrong with selling blood, but with Eric's present weight-loss it had to have made him even more tired.

"I've been looking into selling sperm. A lot of interns do it for extra cash."

Before saying anything, Zac weighed the pros and cons of Eric jacking into a jar for money. "Would it bother you to know there could be a child of yours out there?"

"Hmmm, that's the big question, isn't it?" Eric sighed and rolled to the edge of the bed. He swung back the covers and stood. "I honestly don't think it would, which actually bothers me even more."

"What's the pay like?"

Carol Lynne

"Hold that thought. I need to get my clothes from the laundry room."

Eric disappeared, leaving Zac time to think. He knew it would make Eric's life easier and wasn't that the most important thing? His lover would still be able to make money without putting in all the extra hours. Zac grinned. He wondered if Eric was allowed an assistant in the sperm retrieval process.

Eric walked back into the room, fully dressed except for his socks and shoes. He sat on the edge of the bed and glanced over his shoulder. "It doesn't pay much, but maybe I can combine that with something else."

Zac reached out and pulled Eric back into his arms. He wanted to beg his lover to accept his offer of room and board while finishing out his internship, but he knew he wouldn't convince him. However, there was someone he loved dearly who could convince anyone of anything. "Can you get a couple days off at Christmas? I'd really like to take you home to meet my family."

"You...you want me to meet your family? They're okay with that?"

Zac couldn't resist giving Eric a kiss. "Of course they'll be okay with it. I'm in love for the first time in my life. My mom will be thrilled."

Eric's expression brightened. "It's been a long time since I've been around a family, but I have to work Christmas and Christmas Eve. Dr. Peters asked for volunteers and since I didn't have anyone..."

"You did. You just didn't know it," Zac cut in.

Eric smiled. "Yeah, well, the good news is that Peters gave those of us who volunteered three days off between Christmas and New Year."

95

"Cool. Then we'll wait and go then."

Eric shook his head. "I can't let you miss Christmas with your family. I'll be at work anyway. There's no reason I can't just join you there. Speaking of, where's there?"

"Houston, well, just west of there actually."

Eric's expression suddenly changed. "Oh. Well, uh, I thought maybe it was some place I could drive."

"Hey, don't worry about it. I'll get you a ticket for your Christmas present," Zac offered. He was already imagining Eric playing with his nieces and nephews. He bet his lover would be fantastic with kids.

"Oh, no, I can't let you do that," Eric declined, shaking his head.

"Eric, please don't be this way. I wanna do it. I've already promised Mom I'd be there, but I don't want to go without you."

Eric pulled away and stood beside the bed. "I thought you promised not to ride roughshod over me? I'm sorry, but I can't take your money. If we're gonna do this it has to be on an equal footing. It's my one and only requirement, you know that."

Zac could feel another fight coming on and that was the last thing he wanted. "Fine. I'll just change my ticket to come back a few days early."

Eric bent down and kissed him. "Thank you for at least trying to understand." Eric grabbed his watch from the nightstand and fastened it around his slim wrist.

"You coming back after your shift?" Zac asked.

"I can if you want me to."

"Oh, I want you to. What time?" Zac would have to call Trey for another cooking lesson.

"This is a short day. If I can get out in time, I'll be here around seven, but I can't make any promises."

"No promises needed. Just call when you leave the hospital, and I'll have dinner ready when you get here."

Eric smiled and bent down for another kiss. "You're too good to me."

"Yeah, well, you might wanna withhold judgement until you've tasted it."

"Gotta be better than soup," Eric chuckled as he headed out the door.

* * * *

"Why does everyone keep staring at me?" Zac asked, putting a head of lettuce into his shopping cart.

Trey snickered. "Actually, I think they're staring at us. You've got that moon-eyed I'm-in-love-look, but then they see me and can't figure the two of us together."

"Why do you do that?" Zac asked Trey.

"Do what?" Trey asked, throwing some croutons into the basket.

"Why wouldn't people think the two of us were in love?"

Trey snorted. "Uh, because guys like you don't go in for guys that look like me."

Zac couldn't believe Trey thought so little of himself. "Your family's totally fucked your self-esteem."

Trey laughed. "My family had a lot of help from a string of loser boyfriends." Trey shrugged. "It's okay. I find I don't even miss the sex. Uh, with boyfriends, not with family." Trey gave an exaggerated shudder. "That's...ick."

Zac wrapped an arm around Trey's neck and brought him in for a brotherly hug. "Their loss." He kissed Trey's temple and released him. "You'll find the right guy, and when you do he'll show you just how fantastic you are."

Trey laughed again. "You're just trying to get my Burgundy-sauce recipe."

Zac noticed they were starting to draw a small crowd. "Maybe we should finish and get the hell outta here."

Trey glanced around, eyes big. "Yeah, maybe you're right."

As they loaded the bags into the jeep, Zac turned to Trey. "Ya know, I've got a feeling Cole's gay. Why don't you ask him out?"

"Cole? Cole who?" Trey asked, getting into the front seat.

"Cole Harding, nitwit. How many Coles do you know?"

"Harding? No way, that man's anything but straight as an arrow."

Zac shook his head and started the jeep. "I don't think so."

Trey shrugged. "Even if he was gay, I'd never have the nerve to ask someone like that out."

"What do you mean, someone like that?" Zac pulled out of the parking lot and headed towards home.

"Ya know, blond."

"You got something against blonds?" Zac asked with a chuckle.

"Not really, but they usually aren't down with the brothas."

That made Zac laugh even harder. "You learn to talk like that at Beverly Hills High?"

"You know what I mean," Trey smacked Zac's shoulder.

"I think you're prejudiced against blonds."

"Fuck off. I've just been turned down by enough to have learned my lesson."

Zac watched Trey out of the corner of his eye. His friend's jaw was doing that ticking thing it did when Trey was upset about something. "Hell, I was just teasing."

"It's okay."

Zac decided to drop the subject. "Are you going home for Christmas?"

"What brought that on?"

"Just wondering. I've already got a ticket to Houston, but Eric has to work. Thought maybe if you weren't going home you could take him out to dinner for me. I'd give you some money."

Trey started laughing. "Seriously? You want to pay me to take your boyfriend out on a date?"

Zac pulled into the driveway and cut off the engine. "You're not taking him on a date. Let's make that clear right now."

"Ease off, Conan. It was my turn to kid. Actually, I'm fixing dinner for Kent and Angelo, so I'm sure one more won't be a problem."

"Why isn't Kent going home?" Zac got out and started unloading the groceries.

"Not sure. Something weird's going on with him lately."

Zac had a feeling that something weird was a five-foot-eleven Italian, but he'd been told in no uncertain terms to stay the hell out of it. He put the sacks on the counter. "Okay, I can pretty much figure the salad out, so why don't you give me a rundown on the rest."

Trey pulled out the thick T-bones. "It's easy. Just put these into a plastic bag, pour that bottle of marinade over them and put 'em in the fridge until you're ready." Trey started to say something and shook his head. "Here, give me a piece of paper, and I'll write it down."

Zac gave Trey a pad and pen and sat at the kitchen table with him. "So where'd you learn to cook?"

Trey didn't even glance up from his perfectly penned instructions. "I spent a lot of time with our cook growing up, much to the disapproval of my parents." Trey shrugged. "Water under the bridge as they say."

The expression on Trey's face was heartbreaking. How could such a great guy look so alone? Zac vowed to do something about that. He hadn't told Trey, but Cole set off his gaydar the day he spotted him watching his friend in the hall at school. Zac knew that look all too well. It was the same way he'd watched Eric the night he first delivered a pizza.

"Okay, so this should hopefully win you some more brownie points with your doctor," Trey said, handing over the piece of paper.

Zac took the sheet and nodded. "Thanks." He reached out and squeezed Trey's shoulder. "You're a good friend."

Trey peered down at himself. "Am I dying or something?"

Zac smiled. "No. I just realised I hadn't told you what your friendship means to me."

"Oookay, but if you try to kiss me, I'll punch you."

Zac held his hands up. "Promise. I'll keep my lips to myself." He winked. "For the time being anyway."

* * * *

Eric was dragging by the time he knocked on Zac's door. He was grateful he didn't have to go home and fix a bowl of noodles. Coming home after a long, stressful day to a gorgeous man and a prepared meal, definitely had advantages, maybe Eric should give moving in more thought.

"Hey," Zac greeted. Eric was embraced by two strong arms and kissed thoroughly.

Eric continued to hold Zac even after his lover's arms started to loosen. "Bad day?" Zac asked, hugging him again.

"Not bad, just long." Eric released his hold long enough to shut the door and step further into the living room. "I was turned down for the whole sperm donor thing." It was still embarrassing six hours after being told.

"What? You're a doctor for God's sake."

"Yeah, but I'm not over five-eleven, height-weight proportional." Eric shrugged. "Story of my life. Now my little swimmers aren't even athletic enough to be chosen."

"I'm sorry," Zac commiserated, giving Eric another kiss. "But, since we're already discussing bad news, I've got some of my own. The flights are full. I can't get back from Houston any earlier than what I'd already planned. I talked to Mom thinking she'd just let me off the hook for the whole trip, but it was a no-go."

Eric hated the idea of spending three full days off by himself. "It's okay, you tried."

"But, Trey said he was having a couple of the guys over for dinner on Christmas night if you can get away from the hospital in time. He said to tell you he'd love to have you."

Eric grinned. He knew Trey hadn't asked out of the blue. Even out of town, his lover was still trying to take care of him. He couldn't summon up an ounce of anger, which only proved how deeply he was falling in love.

"We'll see." Eric inhaled. "Something smells good."

"Shit, the steaks." Zac released Eric and rushed into the kitchen.

Eric took off his jacket and hung it in the closet. "I'm gonna change," he called out.

"Okay. Dinner will be on the table in five minutes."

When Eric walked into the bedroom he was surprised to find all of his clothes in neat stacks against the wall. He picked out a pair of shorts and a T-shirt, still marvelling at the kindness of the man in the other room.

He dressed quickly and sat on the edge of the bed. What was he doing? Paying off his student loan had become such a mission that he'd almost let a man like Zac get away. Maybe he could still pay on his loans, but use some of the money to live on? Would it really be so bad if he spent an extra year or two paying loans, especially if he had Zac at his side for those few extra years?

"Eric? Dinner's ready," Zac called.

"Coming." Eric stood and glanced around the room. He could see himself living there, going to bed with the man he loved every night. Yeah, spending the money would be worth it.

Chapter Nine

"Have a good holiday, Dr. Peters," Eric said.

Jules Peters handed Eric a cup of eggnog. "You have big plans for your three days off?" Jules asked, taking a seat beside Eric in the staff lounge.

"No, not really. I'm on for the next forty-eight, so I'll probably just sleep on my days off."

Dr. Peters took a drink. "What happened to that man you were dating?"

Eric flushed. Dr. Peters had never spoken to him about his sexuality. "Um, it's still going, but Zac went home to Houston for the holidays."

"And he didn't ask you to go?"

"No, I mean, yeah, he did, but I don't have the money for the ticket."

Dr. Peters studied at Eric over the top of his glasses. Uh oh. Eric knew that expression. "Dr. Stanton, I know the hospital doesn't pay its interns a king's ransom, but surely you can afford a plane ticket. It's Christmas." He reached out and squeezed Eric's shoulder. "You should be with the people you care about at this time of year."

"I had to quit my part-time job," Eric tried to explain.

"Yes, I thought you might have one of those, which, by the way, I thought I'd made it clear I don't approve of." Dr. Peters finished off his eggnog and set the glass aside. "You remind me a lot of myself at your age, so let me give you a bit of advice. Nothing, and I mean nothing, is worth the love of a good man."

Eric was shocked. The feeling must've shown on his face because Dr. Peters chuckled. "Yes, shhh. I don't make it a habit to spread my sexual preference around. I'm simply telling you so you don't make the same mistakes I made."

"You lost someone because of your career?"

"Not because of my career, more like in spite of my career. I had a good man, much like you do, who was there for me, but I was too busy with work and school." Dr. Peters shook his head. "Morgan was in a wreck and died two years after I finished my residency. It was then that I realised I'd wasted too much time thinking about my career instead of what was really important."

Dr. Peters abruptly stood. "Well, I'm gonna get out of here for a few days." He peered down at Eric. "Do yourself a favour and try to find a flight to wherever your man is. Believe me, someday you'll be glad you did."

Eric stood and shook his boss's hand. "I appreciate the advice. I'll think about it."

Dr. Peters smiled. "Just don't think too long." He gave Eric one last wave before leaving the room.

Eric picked up their cups and dumped them into the wastebasket. Tickets this late would be outrageously expensive even if he could manage to find one. He walked back into the emergency department with a lot of things on his mind.

* * * *

"Hey, baby, grab some paper and start wrapping," Evelyn Grainger ordered, putting a bow on a present.

"Geez, Mom, you buy enough presents?" Zac chuckled. He sat on the bedroom floor beside his mother and reached for a roll of paper.

"Shut up, it's what grandmas do."

Zac picked up a big toy dump truck. "How the hell should I wrap this?" he asked, turning the toy around in his hands.

"Oh, I have a bag for that one." She pointed towards the bed. "I think they're up there. Grab some tissue paper while you're at it."

Zac did as instructed. He found a pen and a tag. "Who's this one for?"

"Robby," Evelyn told him, not glancing up from her wrapping.

They worked side by side for several minutes. Zac had mentioned Eric to her before, but he wanted advice for a change. "I'm trying to get Eric to move in with me," he mentioned casually.

"Really?" Evelyn's cutting paused. "Things are that serious between the two of you?"

"I hope so." Zac finished folding an end and slapped a piece of tape on it. "I'm in love for the first time in my life." There, he'd said it.

Evelyn put the scissors down and launched herself at Zac. He laughed and wrapped his arms around his mom. "I take it that's a good thing," he chuckled.

"It seems like I've waited forever for you to tell me you'd finally found someone special."

"Well he is. Of course I haven't been able to convince him, yet, but I'm still working on it." Each day they were together Zac thought they were getting closer.

Evelyn pulled back and resumed her spot on the floor. "What's the problem?"

Zac started telling his mother about Eric's financial situation using the money he earned to pay off his loans. "It drives me crazy," he finished.

"You have to give the boy credit, though. Not many twenty-somethings care that much about being financially responsible."

Zac's jaw dropped. "Is that a slam at me?"

Evelyn laughed. "No, dear boy, though someday I hope you move out of a garage, and into a real home."

Zac finished the gift he was working on and set it aside. "So tell me how to convince Eric that I can support the two of us until he finishes his training?"

"I can't," Evelyn stated.

"What? You've never been shy about giving your opinions," he snorted.

"To you, yes, but I'm not about to give you advice on your love life. That's a definite no-win situation for me. You and Eric will have to figure it out for yourselves."

"Gee, thanks. I thought I'd at least get some words of wisdom to take back to California with me."

"Nope, but I got you some new socks to take back."

Zac laughed. His mom was famous for telling people what a present was before they even opened it. He covered his ears with his hands and sang. "I'm not listening."

* * * *

"Merry Christmas," Zac greeted.

"Merry Christmas to you," Eric replied. It was only six in the morning and he'd been on shift for almost twenty-five hours. "What're you doing awake so early?"

Zac laughed. "Are you kidding? Hell, we've already opened presents. When you've got kids in the house, you get up at the crack of dawn on Christmas morning."

Eric groaned. "Yeah, I remember those days."

"So how're you holding up?" Zac asked.

Right on cue, Eric yawned. "I managed an hour catnap earlier. I think I'm about due for another though."

"How much longer you got?"

Eric yawned again and looked at his watch. "Twenty-four hours, provided my replacement shows up on time."

"That's insane," Zac commented.

"Yeah, but I knew what I was signing up for when I went into this line of work. Hopefully most people got the partying out of their system for a few days, and I can catch a few hours of sleep later. So what'll you do the rest of the day?"

"Hmmm, Mom's making a big breakfast as we speak. After we get the dishes cleaned up, she'll start on the big Christmas feast. I'll probably spend the day watching movies and taking toys out of their packaging. Have you ever seen how many fucking twist-ties they use nowadays? It's insane. It takes you longer to unwrap the damn things than the kids spend playing with them."

Eric laughed. He envied Zac. His lover may complain, but he could tell Zac loved every moment of being around his family. Eric smiled to himself. He couldn't wait to surprise Zac. Eric heard a woman's voice in the background. "Is that your mom?"

"No, my sister Beth. I guess breakfast's ready."

"Oh, I'll let you go then. Can I call you later?"

"You don't even need to ask. No matter what I'm doing, I'll always be happy to stop and talk to you," Zac replied.

The statement filled Eric's heart. If he'd been the least bit hesitant about the changes he had decided to implement, Zac's words just cemented his resolve. "I love you," Eric declared. He knew he didn't say it enough, but hopefully that would also change in the future.

"I love you too. Miss you."

Eric heard Zac's name called again in the background. "You'd better go. I'll catch up with you later."

"Okay. Try to get some rest."

"I will." Eric hung up the phone and turned it off. Slipping it back into his coat pocket, he left the lounge with a sigh. In less than thirty hours he'd be with Zac.

When he walked back into the emergency department a nurse caught his attention. "Problem?" he asked.

"No. There's a guy named Trey out front that asked to see you if you had time."

"Thanks." He strode towards the waiting room. He couldn't imagine why Trey would be down there so early in the morning. As soon as he walked into the room he spotted the handsome man standing off to the side with a picnic basket in his hand.

"Hi," he greeted, stepping up to the man.

Trey smiled and held out the basket. "I thought I'd bring you some leftovers since you couldn't make it to dinner."

Eric took the basket and gestured towards the consultation room off to the side. "Do you need to rush off or...?"

"No. I'm not doing anything besides going through the sales circulars." Trey followed him into the small room.

Eric didn't shut the door in case someone needed him. "I appreciate you bringing the leftovers. I had a sandwich from one of the machines a few hours ago, but that's about it."

"I figured that." Trey grinned. "Of course it didn't hurt that Zac called to suggest it," Trey chuckled.

"Oh God, I'm so sorry. Did he wake you?"

"Yeah, but I didn't mind. It's nice to see him worry about someone."

Calm overcame Eric. "I'm flying down to Houston as soon as my shift ends in the morning. I thought I'd surprise him. You don't by chance have his folks' number, do you? I'd hate to just show up on their doorstep."

Trey scratched his jaw and shook his head. "I don't, but I know they live in Sugar Land and their names are Jack and Evelyn Grainger. I guess you could always call information."

"I'll try that," Eric said. "Is it okay if I get the basket back to you when I get back?"

"Oh, sure. I don't go on many picnics this time of year anyway."

The pager clipped to Eric's coat pocket buzzed. "Sorry," he apologised, glancing at the display. "Guess it's time to get back to work." He stood and lifted the basket. "Thanks again for bringing this by. Sorry you got stuck with babysitting duty," he said with a grin.

"No big deal. Tell Zac hi when you see him." Trey gave Eric a studying look. "It's good you're going down there. I was starting to wonder."

"Wonder?"

"About how serious you were about him. He's my best friend, and I didn't want to see him hurt."

"I'm serious. It just took me a while to figure out my priorities."

"Good."

Eric said goodbye to Trey and carried the basket back to the lounge, surprised at the weight. Trey must've taken Zac seriously.

* * * *

Movement from the woman beside him woke Eric. He looked around to see passengers standing in the aisle waiting to disembark. "Sorry," he apologised to the older woman.

"That's quite alright, dear, you must've been really tired."

Eric stood and retrieved his bag from the overhead compartment. He couldn't believe he was in Houston already. The last thing he remembered was buckling his seat belt.

When he'd called the Graingers the previous evening, Zac's mom had insisted on picking him up from the airport. Now, as he walked past the security exit, he looked around the crowd of people.

"Eric?" An attractive woman in her early fifties said, approaching him.

"Mrs. Grainger?" he asked back.

The next thing he knew he was enveloped in a hug. "It's so nice to finally meet you," Evelyn announced, squeezing harder.

"Nice to meet you, too. But how did you know who I was?"

Evelyn giggled and pointed towards his hair. "Zac likes to talk about your blond curls. Since you were the only good-looking man who appeared half-dead from exhaustion with blond curls, it was pretty easy."

Eric chuckled and ran his hand through his hair. "I must look frightening. I slept the entire trip."

"Nonsense. You're adorable." Evelyn glanced down at the small rolling bag. "Is that all you brought?"

"Yep."

"Good, then let's get you to Sugar Land. I'm sure Zac's going to be ecstatic to see you."

Evelyn led him to a large four-wheel drive white pickup. "It's not a long trip, but take another nap if you need to."

"No. I'm good for now. So, Zac still has no idea I'm coming, right?"

"Right. I told him I was going to hit a few of the shoe sales, knowing he wouldn't be interested." She winked. "I think I heard him say something about fishing."

"Oh yeah? I didn't know he liked to fish." Eric realised there was a lot of little things he hadn't bothered to learn about Zac. He suddenly felt ashamed. Maybe he should've been spending more time getting to know the man he'd fallen for, and less time trying to figure out how fast he could pay off the exorbitant loan he carried.

"It's not a passion with him the way it is with some folks, but he enjoys it when he's home. We've got a little four-acre pond behind the barn."

Eric remembered Zac mentioning he'd grown up on a hobby-ranch as he called it. Eric couldn't remember the last time he'd been fishing. The thought of doing it with Zac put a smile on his face. "I hope he's still out there when we get there," he commented.

"Oh I'm sure he will be." Evelyn lowered her voice like she was telling a secret. "When he was younger, he used to take his magazines out there with him. He thought I didn't know, but of course I did. I just decided to give him the space he needed until he was comfortable in telling us he was gay."

Eric's gaze swung from the scenery out his window to Evelyn. "You knew even before he said something?"

Laughing, Evelyn reached out and patted his knee. "Of course I knew. All mothers know whether they want to admit it to themselves or not."

Eric's gaze wandered back to the scenery. Had his mom known? If she had, why hadn't she made coming out easier on him?

"Zac told me you don't have a relationship with your parents. I'm sorry about that. Some people don't deserve the kids God blessed them with."

After a few minutes, Evelyn pulled onto a winding gravel drive. "Here we are, home sweet home."

She pulled the truck to a stop. "Why don't you go on back to the pond, and I'll take your bag in."

"Thanks." He could see the pond behind the barn, but there was no sign of Zac. "Are you sure he's still out there?"

Evelyn grinned and opened the door. "I'm sure."

Eric climbed down from the truck and started towards the pond. Once he'd cleared the barn, he began scanning the edges of the pond. It wasn't until he got closer, that he saw the depression in the tall grass that lined the water.

As much as he wanted to run towards his lover, the idea of sneaking up on Zac held more appeal. He pulled the phone out of his pocket and called Zac's number, praying he had his cell on him.

"Hey," Zac's voice greeted.

Eric couldn't miss the deep drawl to Zac's voice. He had a very good idea what his lover was up to. He crept through the waist-high grass towards the edge of the water. "You sound funny, what're you doing?"

"Thinking of you," Zac replied.

"Really? What're you thinking?" Eric felt his cock harden and reached down to unzip his jeans, giving his erection room to grow.

Carol Lynne

"Mmm," Zac moaned. "How nice it'd be to fuck you right about now."

Eric was close enough he could just about make out Zac's form lying on the ground. His lover had his jeans down around his knees and his cock in his hand. Eric smiled, thinking about the condoms and single use lube he had in his jeans pocket. He'd been nervous as hell he'd be pulled out of line at the airport and searched, but it had been worth it.

"What would you say if I begged you to fuck me right now?" he whispered.

"I'd say hop on," Zac moaned again.

Eric watched as his lover's hand sped up. Zac's hips lifted as he thrust into the tight circle of his hand. "Don't come yet," he ordered, continuing to whisper.

"Why, you gonna strip and join me?"

Eric pulled off his shirt and dropped it to the ground. "That's exactly what I'm going to do," he said, coming to a stop right beside Zac.

Chapter Ten

Zac almost swallowed his tongue as he gazed at the hard cock in his lover's hand. Wait a minute. *Fuck.* "What're you doing here?" he asked, reaching up to pull Eric down on top of him.

Chuckling, Eric tossed his phone to the ground and kissed him, tongue pushing in deep. Zac's hands were immediately stripping Eric of his shoes and jeans. "God I missed you," he said, stealing another kiss. "But how'd you get here?"

"I flew and your lovely mom picked me up at the airport," Eric answered, digging out a condom and an individual use packet of lube from his jeans' pocket. "I even came prepared."

Zac held up the lube. "I'll be dammed. I've heard of these, but I can honestly say I've never seen one."

"Yeah, well, I'd prefer you used it instead of just looking at it." Eric reached down and stroked Zac's cock. "You were awfully sexy lying here beatin' your meat."

Zac chuckled. "It's my favourite spot in the world to jack off."

"Yeah, your mom told me."

Zac gasped. "She did not!"

Laughing, Eric nodded. "She did. I think your mom's a lot smarter than you evidently give her credit for."

Zac's head was swimming. How the fuck did his mom know? Hell, he'd been coming down here since he was twelve years old. "I swear I'm scarred for life." Something suddenly dawned on him. "Did she say if she saw me?" Zac covered his face. "I'll never be able to look her in the eyes again."

Eric peppered Zac's face with kisses. "No, she didn't say that she saw you. Evelyn just told me this was where you used to bring your magazines. Did you know she's always known you were gay?"

Zac thought back to the day he'd come out to his family. "I came out to them when I was a senior in high school. We were at the dinner table and my dad asked if I was going to the prom. When I told him no, he wanted to know why." Zac shrugged. "So I told him."

"How'd they react?" Eric asked.

"Dad studied at me for a few seconds, shrugged and said, 'Well I guess that's as good a reason as any'. I couldn't believe it. Of course we didn't tell anyone outside the family. I'd already been given a football scholarship to Idaho, but we didn't want to jeopardise that."

Eric sat up, straddling Zac's hips. "You're lucky."

"I know. I've got a great family." Zac ran his hands from Eric's collarbone down his torso to his cock.

"And an even better boyfriend." He pressed his thumb against the slit at the top of Eric's crown. "We gonna talk about the family or fuck?"

Eric's brow shot up as he reached for the lube. Zac watched his lover tear open the plastic container and squirt the slippery stuff into his hand.

"You gonna just sit there and watch?"

Feeling ornery, Zac nodded. "Yeah, I thought I just might." Zac grabbed the condom and sheathed himself as Eric reached back and groaned. "Turn around. I wanna see you play."

Zac tucked his crossed arms under his head, waiting. He was well rewarded for his patience when Eric turned around. His lover already had two long fingers pushing in and out of his hole. Zac clenched his fingers together to keep from reaching out.

Eric moaned as he inserted a third finger. A bead of sweat dripped down the side of Zac's face as he tried to maintain control. "Fuck," he groaned.

Eric sat up straighter and turned to glance over his shoulder at Zac. "You like that?" Eric asked, riding his fingers.

"You take my breath away." Zac reached down and fisted his cock, the rubber a reminder of where his dick wanted to be. "Need you," he grunted.

With an angelic smile, Eric turned to face Zac once more. Zac held his cock by the base as Eric slowly lowered himself. The squeeze was so intense, Zac prayed he'd last. What better place to make love to the man of his dreams than the spot where they were first created? How many times did he lay beside the lake wishing he had a lover to share it with?

Fully seated, Eric reached down and pinched Zac's nipples. Zac pulled the smaller man down for a deep kiss. Their tongues brushed and duelled until Eric broke the kiss and sat back up. As his lover began to ride him, Zac could see the fatigue in the shadows under Eric's eyes.

Sitting up, Zac wrapped his arms around Eric's waist and turned them over, putting himself in the driver's seat. "Let me make you feel good," he whispered.

He surged deep, relishing the tight squeeze of his lover's inner muscles. As he stared into Eric's eyes, Zac let his emotions take over. His cock wanted to possess the ass it was fucking, imprinting Zac in Eric's heart for life.

The sighs and grunts from the man under him, told Zac he was doing just that, but even if his lover hadn't uttered a peep, Zac would've known by the look in Eric's eyes. This was it, the man he was destined to grow old with. Zac knew that beyond a shadow of a doubt.

He hooked his arms under Eric's knees and spread his lover, plunging in deeper. "I love you," he panted.

Eric didn't say a word, simply nodded, that sparkle never leaving his eyes. The rhythm increased and the sounds of slapping flesh filled the afternoon air. He felt his orgasm begin to build. Zac's hole clenched in anticipation, he suddenly realised he wanted Eric inside of him. Soon, he thought.

"Gonna come," he warned. Zac watched as Eric increased the speed of the hand on his cock.

His breath caught in his chest as his rhythm faltered. He buried his cock as deep as it would go and ground

119

his groin against Eric's ass as he shot into the condom. Eric cried Zac's name and shot his warm seed between them, his lover's ass sucking at Zac's cock like the finest set of lips.

He thrust his tongue into Eric's mouth, swallowing the cries that would alert anyone in the area as to what they were up to. The kiss turned tender as they both came down from their mutual highs. Zac released Eric's legs and cupped the face he'd never tire of looking at. "That's two fantasies you've now gifted me with. I feel like I should be reciprocating. Tell me one of your deepest fantasies."

Eric grinned. "Well, the one I've given most thought to lately isn't an old fantasy at all. It's one I've thought about only since meeting you."

"Hmm, and what's that?"

Eric's cheeks flushed. "I keep wondering what it would've been like if I'd had you as a coach. If you would've been attracted to me? If you would've risked everything to fuck me in the showers?"

Zac closed his eyes and groaned. "I can honestly say I've never been sexually attracted to one of my players, but yeah, I'd risk everything for you."

"Are you boys planning on eating dinner?" Evelyn's voice yelled across the field.

Eric started to giggle and Zac covered his lover's mouth. "We'll be in in a minute, Mom," Zac called back. He returned his attention to the man in his arms. "Ever been swimming in a cold pond?"

Eric shook his head. "No, but I think I'm about to."

"Damn straight. As open as my folks are, I doubt they'd want us coming to the supper table smelling of spunk."

* * * *

By the time Eric was rinsed off and dressed, he was shaking so bad he couldn't tie his shoes. "You know you're gonna have to take care of me when I catch pneumonia?"

Zac chuckled and wrapped warm arms around him. "Promise. Although you're the doctor in the family." He gave Eric a kiss. "Let's get you inside."

Eric let Zac lead him back to the large pale yellow farmhouse. "I'm glad I came," Eric sighed, snuggling against Zac's side.

"I'm glad you did, too. Mind telling me why you changed your mind?"

"Hmm, let's just say a very wise man set me straight on career goals and the grander scheme of things."

"Ooh, sounds mysterious. Does this wise man have piercing grey eyes and a head of thick silver hair?"

Eric glanced up at the man he loved. "Maybe."

Zac opened the back door and walked Eric into the dining room. A large group of people were already assembled around the table. "Everyone, I'd like you to meet Dr. Eric Stanton. Eric, you've already met Mom, this is my dad Jack, my brother Hank and his wife Holly, their kids Robby, Jasper and Gretta, the pregnant lady is my baby sister Beth, her husband Charlie and their kids James, Olivia and Anna."

Wow, how the hell was he going to remember everyone? "Nice to meet you all."

Beth laughed. "Don't worry. We don't expect you to get our names right until you come back for Easter."

Eric chuckled and took a seat beside Zac. He couldn't get over how normal everyone seemed around him. He'd barely met them yet they already treated him like a member of the family.

To prove the point, Hank's wife Holly pointed towards the little guy on Eric's right. "Sorry, but whoever sits next to Jasper gets to help cut up his meat. I hope you don't mind."

"No. I don't mind at all." He picked up his steak knife and wielded it like a scalpel. "Did you know I'm a doctor, Jasper? I cut things up for a living."

Jasper's eyes rounded, his little mouth in the shape of an "O". The whole table started laughing as Eric skilfully cut up the small piece of steak on the boy's plate.

When he finished he began filling his plate. "Everything looks delicious, Mrs. Grainger."

"Call me Evelyn," she insisted.

Eric noticed Zac's father had said very little up to that point. He began to wonder what Jack was thinking. As far as he knew, this was the first time Zac had ever brought someone home with him. Eric swallowed his bite of food and regarded the well-built man at the end of the table. "You've got a nice place here, Mr. Grainger. What sort of animals do you keep?"

Jack swallowed and wiped his mouth. "Just a couple horses, a handful of cattle and more chickens than I care to count." Jack looked at his wife and smiled. "The chickens are Evelyn's thing. I hate the little bastards."

"Jack," Evelyn admonished.

"Sorry," he apologised to the woman and kids at the table. "What I really want to know," Jack began to question, leaning his elbows on the table, "is will you even be around at Easter?"

Eric was taken aback at the question.

"Dad," Zac cut in. "That's between me and Eric."

"That's okay," Eric said, putting a calming hand on Zac's thigh. "I've done a lot of thinking recently, and yeah, I'd like to be here." Zac's hand landed on top of his, threading their fingers together. Eric gazed at Zac. "I love your son, Mr. Grainger. I hope that doesn't cause problems within the family, but I'm not going away."

Zac's father nodded. "That's all I needed to know. And call me Jack."

"Thank you." Eric smiled.

"And thank you," Zac said, kissing Eric's temple.

"We have a lot to talk about," Eric whispered. "Later, though, okay?"

Zac grinned and they resumed their dinner. Eric had no trouble keeping up the conversation. It amazed him how easy the Graingers were to talk to. Yeah, he'd definitely be back.

After dinner, Zac drew Eric outside to sit on the front porch swing. "I love your family," Eric said, snuggling against Zac's side.

"I think the feeling's entirely mutual. In fact, I'm not sure I've ever seen my mother smile so much."

Eric knew it was the perfect time to discuss their future together, but that didn't mean he wasn't nervous. He leaned forward and took his wallet out of his back pocket. "I've been doing some figuring," Eric announced, extracting a single sheet of folded paper.

"Yeah?"

He held the paper up so Zac could read it. "If the offer to live with you is still open, I'd like to propose the following."

"Oh, sounds official," Zac chuckled.

Eric smirked. "I can afford to contribute a third of my pay to the household bills. That will leave a third for loan payments and a third for personal bills. Although I'll still be on the rather shitty schedule I'm presently on until I finish my residency, I promise to come home as soon as my shift ends and not take another job."

Eric folded the sheet and stuffed it back into his wallet. "Of course that dollar amount will go up when my salary does."

Zac chuckled and pulled Eric into his lap. "Honestly? I don't give a damn how much money you give me. Do whatever you need to to make yourself comfortable."

He pulled Eric in for a kiss. "I don't know what Dr. Peters said, and I don't really need to know, but remind me to do something special for him as a thank you."

"Mmm," Eric moaned, sucking on Zac's lower lip. "I'll think on it later."

* * * *

Eric took off his cleats and set them under the bench before starting on the laced football pants. A noise behind him made him smile. "Hey, Coach," he greeted, his cock hardening in the tight white pants.

"What're you still doing here?" Coach Grainger asked him.

He wasn't about to tell his coach what he was really doing there. "I ran a couple extra laps." Eric stood and took off his jersey, tossing it to the bench beside him.

"Everyone else already gone?" Coach asked.

"Yep," Eric answered, bending at the waist to peel his pants down and off. He didn't miss the sharp intake of breath as the man behind him got a glimpse of his puckered hole. His jockstrap was next, allowing his cock to spring back and slap at his flat stomach.

Eric glanced over his shoulder to find his coach rubbing at his crotch. Excellent. He stood upright and slowly turned to face the man of his nightly fantasies. "I'm going to take a shower," he announced, allowing his hand to brush the length of his erection. "You won't turn off the lights on me, will ya, Coach?"

His coach took a step forward, his hand going down the front of his pants. "I might need to watch to make sure you're getting clean, jock itch is a horrible thing."

Eric nodded his head seductively towards the showers. "Good idea. I sometimes have trouble reaching all my nooks and crannies."

Instead of turning on one of the showerheads, Eric turned on three and was quickly enveloped in a cloud of steam. He took the bar of soap and began brushing his chest, fully aware Coach was watching. "Mmm, this feels good," he purred, washing the crack of his ass.

A muscular set of arms encircled his chest as Coach stepped up behind him. Coach took the bar of soap from Eric and ran it down his chest to his groin. "You have to make sure to soap yourself good. Sweat can linger in the tiniest of locations."

Eric reached up and back, looping his arms around Coach's neck. "You saying I have tiny locations?"

The coach dropped the soap to the floor, one hand wrapping around Eric's cock, the other sudsy hand sliding up and down Eric's crack. Coach circled Eric's hole before pushing inside with one large finger. "This is the location that usually needs the most attention," Coach said, biting Eric's neck.

"I've tried cleaning it, but I just can't reach far enough in with my fingers," Eric replied innocently.

Coach inserted another finger, stretching Eric wide with a scissor action. "Bend over and brace your hands on the wall. I think I need a closer inspection." Coach lowered to his knees as Eric bent over and presented himself.

"Yeah, I can see where getting in here far enough to thoroughly clean might be a problem," Coach mused. "Perhaps my tongue would be a better tool."

Eric felt Coach's finger slip free of his hole moments before a tongue lapped at his opening. "Oh, Coach. Yeah, I think that'll work much better."

Coach continued to fuck Eric with his tongue, stopping to nip the sensitive pucker occasionally.

"You know, I might have an even better tool for the job, but you gotta promise me something first."

"Anything," Eric told Coach.

"I think my ass needs a thorough washing when I'm finished with yours. Can you do that?"

Eric's eyes opened, despite the pounding water. Fuck. "Um, I can try. I've never washed anyone like that before." Eric swallowed around the excitement building in his body at the thought of fucking his coach.

The coach picked up the bar of soap and slicked Eric's hole before sudsing his own cock. "I've faith in you, Eric. I've already taken care of the hard part for you," the coach said, slowly pushing his cock deep into Eric's hole.

Arching his back, Eric's body gleefully accepted the invasion. "The hard part?"

"Stretching," Coach replied. "Like all good athletes I never start anything physical without doing a good deal of stretching first."

Eric almost swallowed his tongue. "I look forward to seeing your technique, sir. I'm always interested in new ways to stretch."

Coach gripped Eric's hips and started riding him hard. "Do you have any idea how many times I've watched this tight ass run up and down the field and wanted nothing more than to bury myself in it?" Coach grunted.

"I would've welcomed you," Eric panted. "I'm getting close, Coach."

"No. Think about the plays we went over earlier. I'm almost there." Coach wrapped his arm around Eric's waist. Eric's feet actually left the shower floor as Coach began fucking him like a mad man. It took every ounce of Eric's control not to come. He tried going over the plays from earlier although during the meeting he concentrated more on Coach's cock than the blackboard.

"Eric!" Coach howled as he slammed into him one last time.

As soon as Coach's body stopped quaking, he turned around and got on his hands and knees. "Your turn."

Eric spun around and gasped. A thick, flesh-coloured plug was embedded deep into the man's ass. "Fuck, Zac, I mean, Coach," Eric groaned, momentarily breaking out of their characters.

Zac chuckled. "Pull it out," he ordered.

Eric pulled out the plug and drove his dick in to the hilt. "Oh, Coach. Oh my God," he continued to moan. Never had Eric felt anything like it. The walls of Zac's ass squeezed around Eric's cock like a vise.

It only took Eric a handful of thrusts before his balls began to draw up painfully. "I'm gonna come, Coach."

"Yeah, do it. Ride your coach's ass to the finish."

The first spurt of seed took Eric's breath away. He could feel it surrounding his cock in the enclosed space, making the last thrust glide in to the root. His body shook as he collapsed against Zac's back. "It was everything I've dreamed of and more," he mumbled.

Zac rolled, so Eric was lying across his chest. "Me, too. You were my first, ya know."

Eric's eyes opened as he lifted his head to stare at Zac. "Seriously?"

Zac nodded. "And I plan on you being the only one."

Eric snuggled in, the hot water still filling the room with steam. "I almost came on the spot when I saw that plug in your ass," he chuckled.

"Well I almost came *puttin'* that plug in my ass," Zac laughed.

"Hmmm," Eric sighed, completely sated. "Did I ever tell you about my doctor-patient fantasy?"

* * * *

"I'm out," Zac said, tossing his cards onto the table. "I've been meaning to ask you, Bobby. Do you have any openings for deep-sea fishing on that fancy trawler of yours?"

Bobby tossed two chips into the pot. "Not my boat, remember?"

Zac did. Bobby had run into some rough times a couple years ago and had been forced to sell his pride and joy to his much older, much wealthier brother. "Yeah, sorry, I remember."

"Anyway, to answer your question, yeah, I've got a couple days here and there still open. What did you have in mind?"

"I'm interested in sending Eric's boss out for a couple of hours as a thank you."

"Call," Bobby said, laying his cards face up.

Zac shook his head as he looked down at the Royal Flush. How someone so lucky in cards could be so unlucky in every other aspect of their life, Zac would never understand.

"Shit," Trey cursed, showing a losing hand.

Bobby scooped the pot of chips towards him and began placing them in neat stacks. "Just get me the guy's schedule, and I'll see what I can do."

Eric's knee knocked against Zac's. "I know he's off Thursday, does that work?"

"Yeah, if he doesn't mind going out in the late afternoon. I've already got a morning trip planned for that day."

"Sounds perfect," Zac said. "I'll drop a picnic basket by the boat for him. It is okay to drink Champaign, isn't it?"

"Yeah, as long as he doesn't get drunk and fall over the side. What did this guy do for you anyway?" Bobby asked.

Zac looked at Eric and smiled. "Gave me my future."

SLOW-PLAY

Dedication

Thanks to everyone in my Carol Lynne yahoo group.
You make me smile every morning, especially Silver
and her Good Moaning emails.

Chapter One

"Is this what I pay you to do?"

From his position on the lounge chair, Bobby Quinn opened his eyes and stared up at the silhouette of his brother Brad. God he hated the sonofabitch. "I'm not out on a charter, so you aren't paying me at all."

"So why aren't you out busting your balls to get a charter?"

Bobby sat up and gestured towards the virtually empty marina. "It's Wednesday. Do you see a lot of tourists around?"

Brad made that little sound in his throat Bobby hated. "Could be something to do with the location, or maybe I need to find a captain who's willing to get out and drum up business."

Standing, Bobby's hands clenched into fists. "You threatening me? Your own brother?"

Brad stuck his hands in his designer suit pockets and shrugged. "Half-brother. Besides, it's business."

Bobby knew Brad was lying. It wasn't business at all. Since the day he'd been born, Brad had hated his guts. Was it his fault their mutual father had fucked his secretary and then divorced his wife when his mistress, aka Bobby's mother, turned up pregnant?

From the way Brad treated him, Bobby guessed his half-brother's answer to the question would be a resounding yes. "And just where am I supposed to find people who can afford the prices you're charging for a day out on the ocean?"

Brad shrugged again in that 'I can't be bothered with details' way he had. "That's your problem."

"Is there anything else you need?" Bobby asked, ready for the conversation to be over.

Brad walked around the 1970 Grand Banks trawler. "Nope. Just checking up on my investment, making sure you're doing the required upkeep on her."

"Fuck you," he seethed.

Bobby had spent eight years, and every penny he had, restoring the fifty-foot trawler back to its original glory, only to have Brad swoop in and buy it from the bank when he missed a couple of payments. He knew the only reason his brother had done it was to piss him off. Bobby was left with no choice but to work for Brad in order to care for the boat he'd come to love. *The Gypsy* meant everything to him, and Brad knew it.

"What about your quarters? Are you keeping them clean like I instructed?" Brad asked.

Two seconds away from pushing him into the Pacific Ocean, Bobby climbed down to the main deck and across the gang plank. He heard Brad yelling after him, but he didn't dare turn around.

Bobby stormed his way towards the parking lot and hopped into his rusted 1983 Jeep. He turned off Capistrano Road onto Highway One and headed north. Dammit. He knew Brad would try to get him to move the boat closer to San Francisco, but the bay wasn't where he wanted to be. He liked the open waters of the Pacific, and he sure as hell liked the people of Pillar Point better than the snobs he'd run into in San Francisco.

He had no idea where he was going, until he arrived at Baker Construction. Pulling to a stop, he waved at Bill, the guard on duty, who opened the heavy steal gate to let him pass. He was lucky Kent had room at the back of the lot for him to store his boat. He wove in and out of the various pieces of construction equipment and supplies, until he reached *My Second Chance*.

A 1966 Pacemaker 53' Flush Deck yacht, *My Second Chance* was no where near ocean-worthy. Bobby still had several years, and more than a few thousand dollars, before that particular dream would become a reality.

He parked beside the make-shift scaffolding he and his buddies had erected to hold the old girl upright, and climbed the ladder. Once aboard, Bobby went below deck and looked around. He hadn't done nearly enough work to the old yacht in the two years he'd had her. Of course he knew the reason. He'd had his heart broken when he'd lost *The Gypsy*.

Thinking the emptiness could be replaced, he'd saved his money and purchased *My Second Chance*. As he looked around the salon he realised it hadn't happened. Hell, maybe he should just sell it?

Living and working almost an hour away from where the boat was stored didn't give him enough time to work on it. Bobby picked up his sanding block and began to work on a small section of the woodwork.

Two hours later, he set the block down and picked up a piece of cheesecloth, running it over the smooth mahogany. He felt better than he had in a week. Getting to his feet, he sat in the cracked leather chair and surveyed what he'd managed to accomplish. He knew restoring the interior of the yacht wouldn't get her into the water any faster, but then he didn't have the money to put her into the ocean anyway.

As he studied the small cabin, he took inventory of everything yet to be done. It was liveable the way it was, but liveable had never been good enough before. What was the point of restoring, if you didn't do it right.

His cell phone rang, bringing him out of his thoughts. Bobby reached into his shorts' pocket and looked at the display.

"Hey," he answered.

"Hey, buddy. Eric wanted me to call and make sure everything was still set for Dr. Peters' cruise?" Zac asked.

"Far as I know. Of course, I might not have a job in the morning."

"Shit. Brad?"

"Yeah. Same old, same old."

"He's such an asshole."

Bobby agreed wholeheartedly. "Unfortunately, unless I wanna find another job and place to live, I'm kinda stuck dealing with his bullshit."

Bobby's gaze took in the yacht's interior once again. He knew if it came down to it, living aboard *My Second Chance* was an option, but the thought of completely abandoning *The Gypsy* made him ill.

"Eric's working late at the hospital. You feel like grabbing a bite?"

"I don't know. I'm at Kent's working on the boat, and I've got about an inch of sawdust in my hair."

"Cool. I'll grab some burgers and join you. I haven't been out there since Eric and I met."

Bobby chuckled. "Yeah, well, don't expect to see a lot of changes. I've been too busy lately to get up here very often."

"Don't worry. I won't bust your balls too bad. See ya in about an hour."

Bobby hung up and tossed the phone onto one of the built-in shelves. If he worked his ass off for the next hour, maybe he wouldn't be quite so embarrassed to have Zac see the minimal progress he'd made.

* * * *

Pulling into his circular drive, Dr. Jules Peters was ecstatic to see the cardboard box on his front steps. Finally.

With his 1967 Jaguar idling, he jumped out and snagged the box from the steps before pulling around to the garage. He pushed the remote to the bay closest to the house and drove inside.

Tearing open the plane brown box, he lifted out the prize he'd searched almost eight months for. Giving the shiny chrome and glass headlight a kiss, he carried it over to the black 1956 Jaguar XK140 he'd been restoring for the past seven years.

Jules shrugged out of his dress shirt and began adding the final piece to the jigsaw puzzle that had occupied much of his spare time.

Once the headlight was in and working, he stepped back and studied the classic car. "Breathtaking," he whispered.

His stomach growled, reminding him he'd missed lunch and now dinner. Jules glanced at the clock on the wall. *Damn.* It was nearly nine. He'd have to throw together an egg sandwich and eat while he dictated the day's files he'd brought home with him.

Picking up his shirt and briefcase, he unlocked the door leading into the kitchen. Stepping inside his house, Jules was once again reminded how lonely his personal life was. Over six thousand square feet of living space, and no one but him to fill it, could easily make a guy lonely.

Tossing the briefcase onto the kitchen table, he set about making a quick bite to eat. As he scrambled the eggs for his sandwich, he kept thinking about the shiny black car in his garage. He still couldn't believe the Jag was finished after all the years he'd put into it. When he'd first found the vintage masterpiece, it had been anything but. He'd purchased it for a song, and was grateful he had another project to keep his mind occupied.

Now it was complete, he'd have to look for something else. Too much time to think generally dropped his spirits like a lead weight on the end of a fishing line.

He thought about the afternoon cruise he was supposed to indulge in the next day. It wasn't that he was ungrateful that Eric and Zac had been kind enough to give him the gift, his heart just wasn't in it. How much fun could riding around in a boat be, especially when he had no one to share it with?

As usual, his thoughts slipped to Morgan. His partner had been killed a little over fifteen years earlier. Jules had tried on several occasions to get back into the dating game, but no matter how much he tried, he compared everyone to his first and only love.

He took the eggs off the stove and popped a couple of pieces of bread into the toaster. No sense dwelling on the past, it only made the nights longer.

* * * *

Jules was on his way home from taking his newly completed pride and joy for a test drive, when his cell phone rang. He didn't even need to look at the caller ID to know who it was. No one ever really called but the hospital, especially on one of his rare days off.

"Dr. Peters," he answered.

"Hi, Dr. Peters. This is Bobby Quinn, captain of *The Gypsy*? I hope I'm not bothering you."

The smooth, but seemingly troubled voice in his ear, sent prickles along the back of Jules' neck. "I'm sorry, can you hold on a moment?"

"Sure."

Jules pulled into his drive and parked in front of the house. "Okay, sorry about that."

"No problem. The reason I'm calling is to let you know I'll need to reschedule your cruise this afternoon. The boat's owner wants *The Gypsy* relocated to the bay area, so a cruise won't be much fun until I can get her settled in."

Jules started to answer, but Bobby cut him off with an afterthought. "Unless of course, you feel like an evening cruise around the bay? I should have her ready to go by seven at the latest."

Jules quickly went through his schedule for the next day. He needed to be at the hospital by six a.m., but he doubted an evening cruise would keep him out late. Besides, he'd spent all morning psyching himself up for the considerate gift Eric and Zac had given him. Jules figured he might as well get it over with. He knew it wouldn't be any easier if they rescheduled.

"An evening cruise sounds fine if you don't mind. Where shall I meet you?"

Bobby gave him the name of the new marina. "I'm not sure yet where *The Gypsy* will be anchored, so I'll meet you out front of the clubhouse."

"Sounds fine. I'll see you at seven."

Jules hung up and pulled the Jaguar into the garage. His gaze wandered to the covered car in the first bay. How long had it been since he'd even uncovered Morgan's car? Hell, he knew he hadn't even driven it on the streets for more than eight years. Jules tried to make it a habit to at least start it three or four times a year, but that was it. After all the work he'd put into restoring it after the wreck, he couldn't bring himself to drive it, or sell it. No, selling the 1978 Firebird was out of the question.

Opening the trunk of the Jaguar, he removed the custom made soft cover and put his newest baby to sleep. With his cruise being postponed for several hours, he had time to search the internet for his newest time killer.

Grabbing a beer from the fridge, Jules entered his cavernous office and powered up his computer. His PC, like everything in his house, was top of the line, though he seldom used it.

Skimming through the classifieds, he spotted what he was looking for. Pulling up a picture of a 1952 Jaguar XK120 Roadster, Jules whistled. He enlarged the photo to study the repairs needed. The red leather interior was completely trashed. Jules guessed the owner had stored the vintage beauty in a barn or other shed-like structure. Rust on the side panels had eaten large holes in the body of the car, but that didn't bother him. At least the front grill and headlights seemed to be intact. Jules knew from experience those were the kinds of items that were hard to track down.

The price was a little steep, but he thought he could get the owner down a couple thousand. He compared the money he'd spend on the project to buying a new car. Most men in his financial position bought at least one new car every year. The last vehicle he'd purchased had been the Jag he'd just finished, and that was some eight years or so ago.

Before he could talk himself out of it, he shot an email off to the owner for more information. He continued to surf the ads as he drank two more bottles of beer.

At five-thirty, he shut down the computer and hopped into the shower. He hadn't done anything to get the least bit dirty, but he hoped a nice cool shower would wake him up a bit.

Drying off, he considered backing out of the whole thing. If he'd thought an afternoon cruise would be depressing, he suddenly realised going out on the water in the evening would be even worse. *Shit.*

* * * *

On his way to the marina that Brad had handpicked, Bobby called Zac.

"Hello," Zac answered.

"Hey. Thought I'd call and give Eric a heads-up that I won't be at Pillar Point if he wants to drop off that picnic basket he'd talked about."

"Why, did you head out early?" Zac asked.

"No. I did a lot of soul searching after you left last night."

"Uh oh."

"Yeah, well, I decided to play it Brad's way. At least until I can get my own boat up and running. I realised I wasn't going to be able to do that while living and working so far away."

"So what're you telling me?"

"That I agreed to move *The Gypsy* to the bay area. I'm gonna take my stuff to *My Second Chance* and live there. I think it'll give me a lot more time to work on her."

Zac didn't say anything. Bobby swapped the phone to his other ear. Finally, Zac cleared his throat. "What'll you do when you finish *My Second Chance*?"

"Tell Brad to shove the job up his ass." It was a dream of Bobby's to put his fuckwad of a brother in his place.

"And you'll just walk away from *The Gypsy*?" Zac asked.

Bobby glanced around him. "It's killing me to be on her every day and know she's not mine. I think a clean break is what I need to move on."

"Sorry, man. That sucks."

"Yeah, but I think I'm making the right decision."

Bobby didn't want to tell Zac about the ultimatum Brad had laid down earlier that morning. Shape up or ship out had been Brad's answer to their argument the previous day. Bobby needed the money he'd earn from Brad if he was going to finish his own boat, so he didn't have much choice, but the whole situation left him feeling a bit…adrift.

"I'm getting ready to head under the bridge, so I'll have to talk to you later," Bobby informed his best friend.

"What should I tell Eric to do about the picnic basket?"

"Don't worry. I'll take care of it," he assured Zac.

"Thanks. Call if you need anything."

He slipped the phone into his pocket and thought about the evening cruise. Although both Zac and Eric spoke highly of Jules Peters, Bobby withheld judgement. He wasn't easily impressed, even less so with wealthy people. He tried to figure out what he could afford to feed the good doctor that would be suitable.

Most cruises on *The Gypsy* were catered affairs, but then for the price Brad charged per hour for the trawler's rental, he wouldn't expect anything less. Bobby's favourite groups to take out were the family reunions, or college buddies getting together for the weekend. At least those people knew how to drink normal beer and eat regular food. But those groups were usually booked by him, and he hadn't been motivated lately to drum up business for Brad.

By the time he reached the marina, his mood was so soured he almost felt sorry for Jules Peters, and he still had to come up with something to feed the man. He'd grab a bottle of mid-priced champagne, the drink of the wealthy, but no way could he afford anything like caviar or smoked salmon. Hell, he'd be lucky to afford a good can of tuna fish.

He spotted Brad standing in front of one of the slips with his hands in his suit pockets. *Fuck. Could my day get any worse?*

Chapter Two

Bobby watched as a shiny black Jaguar pulled into the parking lot. He whistled, thinking of the money it would cost to even maintain such a vehicle. A man dressed in khaki slacks and a sports shirt climbed out of the car and began walking his way.

He had to admit his cock did a little thump against the front of his jeans. Rich or poor, the man was hot as hell. It was easy to imagine the guy strolling into the club to meet his fellow yacht buddies. Bobby bet the guy had one of those wives who'd been stretched and pulled until she could no longer close her eyes.

Chuckling to himself, he was surprised when the fine piece of upper crust walked up to him.

"Captain Quinn?"

Captain? No one ever called him that. "Uh, yeah, I'm Bobby Quinn."

"Nice to meet you, I'm Jules Peters."

Bobby's cock lengthened further. This was Dr. Peters? It didn't help the situation any knowing the man was gay. *Damn, Zac.* Was his friend trying to play matchmaker?

"I hope I'm not too late. I had trouble with the car on the way over."

Bobby realised Jules had his hand extended. "Oh, sorry, no you're fine."

He gestured towards the Jaguar. "Beautiful car."

Jules stuck his hands in his pockets, his gaze moving back towards his car. "Yeah. I thought I was finished working on it, but it kept dying on me on the drive over."

Bobby glanced at Jules' hands. No way had those clean hands ever done any engine work. He assumed Jules must be referring to his mechanic. Deciding to change the subject, he pointed behind him. "You ready?"

"Sure," Jules said, adjusting his mirrored sunglasses.

Bobby led the way to *The Gypsy*, allowing Jules to climb the gangplank first. Customer service was part of his job. It had absolutely nothing to do with wanting a peek at the man's ass. *Yeah, you keep telling yourself that.*

"Wow, great trawler," Jules admired, looking around the deck.

Bobby was impressed. Most people didn't know a trawler from a pontoon. "Thanks. I restored her myself."

"Oh, so it's your boat?" Jules asked.

"No," Bobby clipped, going below to get the wine. He didn't know why he let the question bother him so much. He'd been asked the same question on almost every charter he'd taken out.

"Make yourself comfortable. I'll just be a moment," he called up to Jules.

After arranging some miscellaneous fruits and cheeses on a tray, he opened the bottle of wine he'd decided on, the fact that the wine had been on sale had nothing to do with it. *Yeah right.*

Carrying the tray up the steep staircase, Bobby set it on a table. He didn't immediately see Jules and turned in a circle until he spotted him. With his hands still in his pockets, the man stood gazing out at the sunset, the bay breeze riffling his short silver hair.

Bobby suddenly wished he had a camera in his hand. The way the setting sun bathed Jules in colour was breathtaking. "I hope wine is okay? Eric didn't tell me what you liked to drink."

Jules jumped a little and turned towards Bobby. "That's fine. I usually drink beer, but I've been known to enjoy a good glass of wine from time to time."

Bobby poured a glass and held it out. Jules seemed to hesitate before reaching for his drink. Was it Bobby's imagination or did Jules take extra care not to touch him?

Jules lifted the glass to his mouth just as the cell phone attached to his waistband began to ring. Jules seemed startled by the intrusion and almost spilled his wine.

What the hell had the guy so jumpy? Bobby wondered.

"Sorry, I have to take this." Jules set the glass down and unclipped the phone.

"Dr. Peters," Jules answered, walking away from Bobby.

Bobby couldn't hear much of the conversation, but from what he did make out, he was glad he hadn't started the boat.

Jules shut the phone and returned it to its case. "Sorry. There's been a massive pileup on the 280. The hospital needs all the help they can get."

Jules shrugged. "The life of a doctor."

"I understand."

Jules glanced down at the big tray of food. "I'm sorry to put you to so much trouble for nothing."

Bobby waved Dr. Peters' concerns away and dug out a business card from his wallet. "Call me when you wanna reschedule."

Jules wiped his hand on his pants before taking the small piece of paper from Bobby. "I appreciate that. Will you still get paid if I leave? I mean, I don't know if I'm supposed to give you a tip or what."

Dr. Peters ran his hand over the back of his neck. "I'm making an ass out of myself, aren't I? It's been awhile since I did anything but work on cars. I'm afraid my social skills leave a lot to be desired."

Bobby could see the man struggling, so he decided to give him a break. Yeah, it sucked that he wouldn't get paid, but there were worse things in life. "Don't worry about it. Really. Just give me a shout when you get a free minute to take a cruise."

After several moments, Jules nodded. "Okay, well, I'd better get going. I just hope my car gets me across town."

Bobby knew in his gut he was going to regret it, but he couldn't help but to offer. "I could give you a lift. As you can see, I don't have much else to keep me busy."

He thought Jules was about to take him up on his offer, but then Bobby made the biggest mistake of the day. He dropped his hand and without thinking brushed the front of his jeans. Jules gaze automatically followed the movement, his eyes going wide at the erection still pressing against Bobby's fly. *Fuck.*

"That's okay. I'll keep my fingers crossed that it makes it back to the house and just switch cars. I'd hate to leave it overnight in a parking lot anyway."

Bobby wanted to crawl under the table beside him. "Okay, thought I'd offer. If you find yourself stalled somewhere, you've got my number."

He waved as Jules left. Zac was going to kill him. Bobby wondered if Jules would tell Eric what a perv Zac's friend was. Flopping down into a chair, he plucked a grape from the tray and popped it into his mouth.

Maybe he'd pack everything up and start moving his stuff over to his boat. *Shit.* He remembered he didn't even have a mattress. Although his berth was one of the few things he'd finished, he'd never bothered with bedding.

Bobby drummed his fingers on the table as he sipped the glass of wine. He could sit here, get sauced and buy a mattress in the morning, or he could put the food away and run to the store.

Studying the pristine marina with all its big sailboats and yachts, Bobby suddenly wanted out. This was Brad's world, not his.

Decision made, he corked the bottle of wine and put the fruit into small plastic bags. Spending another night on *The Gypsy* was no longer an option and Bobby knew it.

* * * *

By the time Jules made it to his car, he was breathing heavy. It wasn't the exertion of crossing the parking lot, it was the attraction he felt for Bobby. Not since Morgan had he been so physically turned on by someone.

Damn. If only he was fifteen years younger. Men like Bobby enjoyed playing, but rarely did he find one who was seriously looking for a boyfriend. It took several tries and several prayers to get the Jag started, but eventually the engine came to life. He knew what the problem was and it was actually an easy fix, but he didn't have the time or the tools at the moment.

Jules made a mental note to buy small toolboxes for each of his cars. He had one in the Jaguar he normally drove, but hadn't thought he'd need one in the show piece he was currently driving.

Pulling out of the parking lot, Jules thoughts drifted back to Bobby. He knew the guy was either attracted to him or perpetually horny. No way could the hard shaft trapped behind those jeans mean anything else. *God, but he's so young.*

Three blocks from the marina, the Jag started to sputter. Jules managed to get the car to the right hand side of the road before it died. Turning off the engine, he rested his head on the back of the seat. *What now?*

Calling a cab wasn't a problem, but no way could he leave a hundred-thousand dollar car on the side of the road. Unclipping his cell phone from his waistband, Jules called the hospital to tell them he'd be late.

He was just about to call for a tow-truck when an old Jeep pulled up behind him.

"Trouble?"

Jules closed his eyes and took a deep breath. When he opened them, Bobby's hands were resting on the driver's door. "Yeah. I was just about to call for a tow."

"Ooh, I wouldn't even trust my Jeep to a tow driver around here. Can I make another suggestion?"

"I'm all ears," Jules replied, trying his best not to look at the gorgeous man beside him.

"Let me call my friends. We can push your car into one of these parking lots and see if we can't get her running."

Jules nodded. "I'd appreciate that. I'm pretty sure it's the sparkplugs. If I had the time, it wouldn't be a problem to swap them out, but every minute I'm here, I know someone in the ER isn't getting my care."

Bobby pulled out his cell phone and started calling his friends, while Jules contacted the hospital once more. He was informed that several of the injured had been rerouted to another hospital. Jules was still needed, but the situation wasn't as dire as they'd first feared.

Jules breathed easier as he waited for Bobby to finish his calls.

"Okay, we're all set. Eric was called in as well and will swing by here and pick you up on his way."

"Thanks."

Bobby waved his hand like it was no big deal. "We'll get your car running again, don't worry."

Jules couldn't believe Bobby was being so nice about the situation. Although he was able to admit to himself he didn't let people in, it felt odd for a near-stranger to so readily offer help.

Kent was the first of Bobby's friends to arrive. After introductions were made, Kent helped Bobby push the car into the nearest parking lot with Jules behind the wheel. Once the Jaguar was off the street, Jules felt much better.

"I can't tell you how much I appreciate this," Jules said, shaking Kent's hand.

"No big deal. I was just sittin' home watching the game anyway."

A new BMW pulled into the lot and a well-dressed business man joined them.

Kent threw up his hands. "What the hell, Angelo. How're you supposed to help us wearing a suit?"

"Excuse me, Mr. Construction Guy, I was just finishing up a business dinner when Bobby called. Would you rather I'd gone all the way home to change?"

Kent rolled his eyes. "I doubt you have anything in your closet that you'd willingly get dirty anyway."

The guy turned away from Kent's sarcasm and extended his hand. "Hi, I'm Angelo Pillato, a friend of Bobby's."

"Nice to meet you. I'm Jules Peters."

"Pay no attention to Kent. He enjoys giving me a hard time." Angelo shrugged. "I've learned to brush off his comments over the years."

Angelo grinned and leaned forward. "He's a lousy poker player, by the way."

"That's bullshit and you know it," Kent blustered.

Another man arrived right before Zac and Eric pulled up. Jules was introduced to Trey. He shook the small man's hand. "Nice to meet you."

"Where's Marco?" Kent asked.

Bobby shook his head. "Out, I guess. His phone went directly to voicemail."

"Figures," Kent grumbled.

"You ready, Dr. Peters?" Eric asked, getting into the driver's seat.

Jules turned towards the men studying the Jag's engine. "Do you know how to change the plugs? If you need tools…"

"No, we got it. Just go and save the world, and we'll deal with your car," Bobby answered with a smile.

Jules nodded his gratitude and climbed into the passenger seat of Eric's small car. "I appreciate this."

Eric grinned and drove towards the hospital. "So, did this screw up your cruise?"

"Yeah. We hadn't even made it out of the marina before I got the call."

"Ouch. That sucks."

"You like boating?" Jules asked.

Eric shrugged. "I don't know, never done it, but it sounds fun."

Jules saw an opportunity and grabbed it. "Well maybe when I call to reschedule, you and Zac can come along."

Yeah, strength in numbers. If he had someone besides Bobby to focus on, maybe he wouldn't make such a fool of himself.

"Really? Yeah, I'd like that. Although I'm not sure when the three of us will be off work at the same time."

Jules let the subject drop.

They drove for another ten minutes before Eric asked, "What did you think of Bobby?"

"Umm, he seems like a nice guy, but then, all your friends seem nice." He hoped that worked. No way did he want Eric to pick up on the attraction he felt for the muscular dark-haired man.

"Yeah, they're great, but Bobby's the best. Did you know he restored *The Gypsy* all by himself?"

"He mentioned it."

"It took him years. Then his brother bought it out from under him once it was almost finished. According to Zac, it broke Bobby's heart."

"I would imagine it would. How did his brother manage to buy it?"

"Bobby was working for Kent at his construction company in order to earn enough to finish the boat. Bobby was hurt on the job, nothing serious, but he was laid up long enough that he missed several payments. The bank was about to repossess, when Brad, that's Bobby's brother, stepped in and bought the loan."

Jules couldn't imagine how much that had to have hurt. "But he finished the boat anyway?"

"Yeah. *The Gypsy* was Bobby's obsession, I guess. He told Zac he'd put too much of his heart and soul into her to walk away. That's the reason he takes the shit he does from his brother. Brad lets Bobby live and captain *The Gypsy*, in exchange for ninety percent of the money and Bobby kissing his ass."

After the conversation, Jules had an entirely different opinion of Bobby. Yeah, the guy was young, but it sounded like he was loyal to a fault, even if it was to a boat. Maybe he needed to go over his calendar when he got home and try and reschedule.

Jules mentally shook himself. Just because the guy was loyal to a boat didn't mean he was ready for a relationship. Jules had occasionally played around after Morgan's death, but it always left him feeling worse than being alone.

He quickly dropped the idea of looking at his calendar. Jules knew he was better off at home by himself, working on his cars. They gave him a sense of peace and accomplishment that sex never did.

As soon as Eric turned into the parking lot, Jules' mind pushed everything to the side as he mentally prepared for the night ahead.

* * * *

Bobby tossed the empty beer bottle into the recycling bin as Zac hung up the phone.

"Eric's on his way home with Jules."

Bobby glanced at the clock on the wall. It was one-thirty a.m. How the hell was he going to get up for work in the morning?

"You told Eric that we brought Jules' car back here?"

"Yeah. Jules understood. Since we couldn't get hold of him to find out his address, we didn't have much choice."

Bobby had been chosen to drive the Jaguar to Zac's place, and his body still thrummed with the excitement. Never in his life did he think he'd be allowed to drive a car like that. The problem was that he had no ride to get back home. Goddammit, he should've argued with Zac when his friend convinced him to drive doc's car back to his place. "You think you or Eric can get me back to the marina?"

"Sure, although I imagine Jules would be more than happy to give you a lift after you fixed his car."

Bobby shook his head. "Naw, I don't know the guy well enough to ask him to do that."

Zac chuckled. "I don't think it's much out of his way. He lives up north in Forest Hill."

Bobby whistled. That was a pretty swanky neighbourhood in the Twin Peaks area. Either Jules made more money than he'd thought, or the man came from money. Bobby realised the assessment wasn't fair. After all, his dad had a ton of money, but that didn't mean he gave Bobby any, not that he would ever ask.

They finished their beer and watched television until the door opened with a tired looking Eric walking over to plop onto Zac's lap.

"I'm beat," Eric groaned, snuggling against Zac's chest.

Bobby's gaze fixed on an equally tired looking Jules. He stood and dug the keys out of his pocket. "You were right. We changed two of the plugs and she started right up."

He could tell Jules was out of it when he didn't even reach for the keys. "Guess I'd better get going then," Jules said around a yawn.

"Are you sure you're okay to drive?" Bobby asked.

"No, but I'll do fine once the wind hits me."

Bobby didn't like the sound of that. "Why don't you let me drive you as far as the marina? We'll see how awake you are by then."

"I could call a cab," Jules mumbled.

"Nonsense, I need to get home anyway, no reason I can't drive you that far. If nothing else, you can call a cab from the marina."

Jules didn't protest further. He simply nodded and turned to head out the door. Bobby glanced at Zac. "I'll see ya Saturday night. Thanks for the help."

"No problem." Zac cleared his throat, pointing towards the empty doorway. "Don't let him do anything foolish."

"Don't worry, I won't."

By the time Bobby got down the steps, Jules was sound asleep in the passenger seat. He smiled at Jules' slightly parted lips and soft snores before starting up the engine. Jules shifted in his seat when Bobby pulled out of the drive.

The doctor's blue eyes opened as he ran a hand over his bristled jaw. "Sorry."

Without thinking, Bobby reached over and put a comforting hand on Jules' thigh. "Don't worry about it. Go back to sleep."

Jules' hand covered Bobby's as he drifted back off. Driving down the highway, Bobby enjoyed the feel of the muscled leg under his palm. It may have started as nothing more than a friendly gesture, but it had soon perked Bobby's cock up.

He was in serious discomfort by the time they reached the marina. Bobby pulled into a parking spot and gave the thigh under him a squeeze. "Jules?"

When Jules didn't move, Bobby tried again, this time giving the man a gentle shake. "Jules? Can you wake up?"

Jules mumbled something Bobby didn't understand, and moved Bobby's hand closer to his crotch. Fuck.

Bobby removed his hand and climbed out of the car. He paced beside the vintage automobile for several moments while trying to keep his lust in check.

Okay, it's pretty obvious the man can't drive home, but he already said he didn't want his car in a parking lot all night. Hell, Bobby didn't blame him a bit. The way he saw it, he only had one choice. He needed to drive Jules home.

Getting back into the car, Bobby shook Jules again. "I need an address. Can you tell me where you live?"

Jules opened his eyes and rattled off an address before closing his eyes again.

"Time to get you to bed." Bobby realised what he'd said and felt his cock knocking against his fly once more. Bobby gave his erection a thump and headed towards Jules' house.

He could always call a cab to take him back to the marina. He knew Zac wouldn't mind doing it, but he was positive his best friend was already in bed. Having grown up in the area, Bobby had no problem finding Jules' house.

Pulling into the circular drive, Bobby was impressed. The stone house looked like no others in the neighbourhood. "Jules?"

Jules eyes fluttered open. "Yeah?"

"Where should I park your car?"

Jules rubbed his eyes and sat up in the seat. "Huh?"

"Your car? Do you want me to just park it, put it in the garage, or what?"

Jules seemed surprised he sat in his own driveway. "You didn't need to drive me home."

"Uh, yeah, I kinda did. You wouldn't wake up when we got to the marina."

Jules covered his face with his hands. "Shit, I'm sorry."

"That's okay. Just tell me where I should park your car." Bobby was starting to get frustrated, it was past two in the morning and he had an eight a.m. charter.

Jules reached under the seat and pulled out a garage door opener. "Continue around to the side of the house. It'll be the last bay on the left."

Bobby put the car into gear and drove around the corner of the house. Sitting back a little from the front of the house was a four-car garage. Jules pushed the button on the opener and Bobby settled the 1956 Jaguar into its parking spot.

As he climbed out of the car, a yawn escaped him.

"Would you like to crash in one of the spare rooms? I can run you back to the marina after you catch a few hours of sleep?" Jules asked.

Although he knew he'd probably regret it, Bobby yawned again and nodded. "Thanks. I'd appreciate that."

Chapter Three

A knock on the door woke Bobby. He blinked his eyes several times and tried to focus on the clock, six. Wanting nothing more than to roll over and go back to sleep, the second knock had him sitting up. "I'm awake."

"I'll be downstairs with a cup of coffee waiting for you. Feel free to shower, towels are under the sink," Jules called through the door.

Bobby scratched the stubble on his face and neck. His normal five o'clock shadow was quickly turning into a beard. If he were at Zac's or one of his other friends, he would've asked to borrow a razor, but he didn't know Jules well enough.

Kicking off the covers he shuffled his way into the bathroom. From what he'd seen hours earlier, the house was massive. He couldn't help but compare it to Brad's house.

Although there was definitely a mutual attraction between him and Jules, Bobby doubted he could let it go anywhere. Money made him nervous, and Jules seemed to have more than his share.

After a quick shower, Bobby pulled on his dirty clothes and made his bed. He assumed Jules would want to wash the sheets, but it would be rude to leave a mess. Out in the hall, Bobby followed his nose down the stairs to the kitchen.

Jules sat at the table with a stack of folders in front of him, a small pair of reading glasses perched on the end of his nose. He glanced up when Bobby entered. "Sleep well?"

Bobby chuckled and headed for the coffee pot. "Like the dead. Of course another couple hours wouldn't have hurt."

"I know what you mean." Jules took a sip of coffee and gestured to the chair across from him. "I'm sorry I don't have much in the way of breakfast foods. I usually just grab some fruit on my way out the door."

"No problem." Bobby blew on the hot beverage before taking a drink.

"Will you have time to run me to the marina, or should I call a cab?" Bobby asked, taking the offered chair.

"I wouldn't hear of it. After everything you've done, the least I can do is drop you off."

Jules took off his glasses and set them on the table. "I really do appreciate you helping me out, both with the car and the drive home. If you ever need anything, don't hesitate to ask."

"It was no trouble, really." Bobby tapped his foot as he finished his coffee. He hated to hurry Jules along, but with an early charter, he still needed to get back and ready the boat.

Jules grinned. "Is that your foot?"

Bobby sheepishly tucked his feet under his chair. "Sorry, nervous habit."

Jules stood and took his empty cup to the sink and rinsed it out. "Let me gather these files, and I'll be ready."

Bobby finished his coffee while watching Jules out of the corner of his eye. Damn, the man was sexy. Every movement seemed to have grace and purpose. Bobby bet the good doctor was amazing in bed.

Damn. In no time, his fantasies had his cock hard as a rock. He reached under the table and kneaded the bulge in his jeans. The more he tried to adjust himself, the harder he became.

A soft sound from Jules got his attention. Bobby glanced up to see Jules staring straight at him with heavy-lidded eyes. *Shit.* It was obvious the man knew what he was doing with his hand under the table.

When Bobby met Jules' blue stare, the doctor quickly turned away. "Well, then, I'm ready when you are," Jules announced.

Bobby knew he had two choices. He could either act on the rod in his pants or ignore it and hope Jules didn't question him about it. The uneasy way Jules fluttered around the kitchen told Bobby it would be best to ignore it.

He stood and rinsed his cup in the sink. "Ready."

Without turning to look at Bobby, Jules picked up his briefcase and headed towards the garage. Bobby couldn't help himself. He stared at the fine ass in front of him until he stepped into the garage.

"We'll take this one," Jules said, getting in the newer Jaguar.

Bobby shook his head as he squeezed his broad muscled frame into the small interior. *Must be nice to have your choice of cars to drive.* Bobby stretched the seatbelt across his chest and searched for the buckle.

Jules' hands suddenly joined his. "Here it is," Jules whispered, clicking the buckle into place.

Raising his head, Jules mouth was a mere inch from Bobby's. God, how much could one man take? The two of them held the position for several long moments before Jules closed the gap.

Soft lips brushed across Bobby's, eliciting a moan from somewhere deep in his chest. Bobby opened up, and ran his tongue over Jules' bottom lip. Within seconds, Jules' hand crept to the back of Bobby's neck as they plundered each other's mouths.

Bobby reached down and released his seat belt as he leaned into Jules' lithe body. Finished with the buckle, Bobby's hand wandered to the erection pressing against Jules' suit pants.

Jules broke the kiss, gasping for air as Bobby began to unzip the doctor's fly. Jules tilted his head back as Bobby's teeth scraped the sensitive flesh of his neck.

With one misplaced elbow, the horn honked, making both men jump. Jules' eyes rounded as the haze of lust lifted. He sat back in his seat and quickly reached down to fasten his slacks. "I'm sorry. Ummm...I can't."

Bobby took a deep breath and settled back into the passenger seat. "Yeah, you're right, it's not a good idea."

"It's just that, well, my life is really hectic, and I don't have time to…oh hell." Jules opened the garage door and started the car.

Bobby kept his attention on the passenger window, afraid to see the remorse in Jules' expression. It was bad enough to hear it in the man's voice, he didn't think he could handle seeing it in those gorgeous blue eyes.

The ride to the marina was uncomfortable to say the least. When Jules pulled to a stop, Bobby practically jumped out of the car. "Thanks for the ride."

"No, thank you for everything you've done."

Without another word, Bobby practically ran to *The Gypsy*. He only had twenty minutes to relieve the ache in his jeans and get ready for his guests. The way his constrained cock throbbed, Bobby figured he had plenty of time.

* * * *

By the time Bobby arrived for Saturday night poker, he was starving, as usual. He lifted a small grocery sack out of the back of his Jeep and ran up the steps. It had been a brutal couple of days, and he was ready for a bit of fun.

Turning the door handle, Bobby walked into Zac's house as he always had and stopped short. "Oops."

Zac quickly pulled his hand out of the front of Eric's pants. "Don't you know how to knock?"

Bobby shrugged. "Sorry, I forgot you actually had a social life now. It won't happen again."

Grocery sack in hand, Bobby retreated to the kitchen to give the two love birds some privacy. He heard Zac chuckle at something Eric must've said, seconds before Eric's cute face peered around the corner.

"I've got to head in to the hospital. Don't take all his money," Eric informed Bobby.

Bobby paused in opening the cookies to laugh. "Easier said than done. Zac sucks at poker."

"I do not," Zac protested, wrapping his arms around Eric.

Eric rolled his eyes and turned his head to give Zac another kiss. "You kinda do, babe, but I love you anyway."

The remark earned Eric a nipple twist. "Ouch."

"I'll kiss it better later. What time will you be home?" Zac asked.

"Not 'til morning. I'm covering for someone. I'll make sure and wake you when I get in."

"You'd better." Zac gave Eric one last kiss before the smaller man left.

Turning to Bobby, Zac put his hands on his hips. "So why are you here so early?"

Bobby opened the package of chocolate chip cookies and stuffed one into his mouth. "I'm not that early."

Zac seemed to study him for several moments. "Something going on?"

God, where should he start? "No."

Not only had he spent the last two days thinking of Jules and the feel of the man's cock in his hand, but he was due to have lunch at his parents' house the following day. When his mom had phoned, Bobby readily agreed. It wasn't until after he'd told her he'd be there that she informed him Brad and his family would also be in attendance. Sitting across the table from Brad would be pure torture, as usual.

"Have you talked to Jules since we fixed his car?"

Bobby popped another cookie into his mouth in lieu of answering.

"Bobby? What's going on?"

"Nothing. Man, what's with the twenty questions?" Bobby tossed the sleeve of cookies on the counter and walked towards the living room.

He was saved from further probing when Marco burst into the house, filthy as usual.

"Hey," Marco greeted. He held up a change of clothes and gestured to the bathroom. "You mind?"

Zac rolled his eyes. "You know the rules."

"Yeah, yeah, clean the bathtub when I'm finished." Marco strode into the bathroom and closed the door.

"Why do you let him do that?" Bobby asked.

"Same reason I let you come over and get crumbs all over my floor. You're family."

"Aahhh." Bobby walked over and gave Zac a kiss on the cheek. "You're so sweet. Of course that doesn't mean I'm going easy on ya. I'll still take your money."

"You wouldn't be my Bobby if you didn't."

Bobby took off his shoes and stretched out on the couch. He heard the shower turn on as he reached for the remote. Marco hadn't been around much in recent months. Besides their semi-monthly poker games, Bobby hadn't even heard from him.

"Kent still have Marco working down south?" he asked.

Zac paused in the act of putting the leaf in the table. "I don't know. I haven't talked to him in awhile."

"Me neither. You think he's got another sugar daddy he's been spending time with?"

Zac finished with the table and walked into the living room. "Your guess is as good as mine. But between you and me, I hope not. Things between him and Kent are tense enough as it is. You know how he gets when Marco is seeing someone."

"Yeah, well the problem is Marco never brings any of them here. Maybe if he didn't sneak around so much, it wouldn't bother Kent to the extent that it does."

"I doubt it. Kent wouldn't be happy regardless."

"He loves Marco," Bobby reminded Zac.

"Of course he does. The problem is he also can't stand him."

"Who can't stand who?" Marco asked, walking out of the bathroom, his hair still dripping water on his bare chest.

"No one," Bobby quickly covered.

Trying to think fast, he came up with a plausible excuse for what Marco had overheard. "We were talking about Brad."

Marco made a face. "Sorry, man, but your brother's a pretentious asshole."

"Don't I know it. And lucky me gets to have lunch with him and his perfect little family at my parents' in less than eighteen hours."

"Ooh, you have my sympathies." Marco wandered back into the bathroom and closed the door.

Zac's eyebrow rose. "Good save."

"Yeah, luckily my life is fucked up enough I can always come up with shit like that." Bobby closed his eyes and clasped his hands together, letting them rest on his chest. He wasn't tired, he just couldn't take Zac's piercing gaze any longer.

"You like him, don't you?" Zac asked after several moments.

"Who?" Bobby asked without opening his eyes.

"You know who I'm talking about."

"His house reminds me of Brad's."

"So?"

Bobby shrugged. "I don't fit into that world."

"Bullshit, you grew up in a house twice the size of Brad's."

"And I was booted out the day I graduated from high school."

Bobby opened his eyes. "In my experience, people with money are only interested in two things. How to earn more of it, and their public image. I don't exactly fit into either category."

"You are so full of shit. You and I both know you have the face and body of a fucking Adonis, it's your mouth that gets you in trouble."

Tired of being held under a microscope, Bobby got up and walked into the kitchen. He pulled a beer out of the sink and brushed off the ice. Being gay in his parents' circle of friends was not acceptable. Growing up, he'd had two choices, learn to suffer through the endless debutant balls, or come out of the closet. His parents had treated his confession as a personal attack on them. Although they'd somewhat made up over the years, the subject of Bobby's preferences were not allowed in their home.

Trying to get his mind off his parents and Jules, he opened the cupboard and found the big plastic bowls Zac used for poker night. Reaching into the sack of junk food he'd brought, he was surprised when Zac's arms circled his waist.

Zac gave him a hug. "You're one of the finest men I know, Robert Orlando Quinn, and don't you forget it."

For a few brief moments, Bobby relished Zac's comforting embrace. Although nothing sexual had ever happened between the two of them, Bobby loved the big lug. "Why can't I be attracted to a normal guy?"

"I don't know, I kinda think you are."

Bobby craned his neck to look up at Zac. "There's nothing normal about Jules."

"Why, because he has money? Being kind of a reverse snob, aren't you?"

Was he? Yeah, he knew he was, but his experiences with wealthy people hadn't been the best. Which is why it still didn't make sense to him that he held a job catering to the rich sons-of-bitches.

If he had his way, he'd cut the charter rates dramatically and get more families on board. "I need to finish my boat."

"Okay. I'm free most evenings to help. Just tell me when and where."

Bobby spun in Zac's arms to face him. "Really? What about Eric?"

"Eric works a lot, and when he's not, he's usually sleeping. I'm not saying I can be on call every minute, but I think I have enough spare time to help a friend. Besides, summers only, like, a month and a half away. Other than the odd football thing, I've got nothing else to do."

"Something you guys would like to tell me?" Kent asked, stepping into the kitchen.

Zac rolled his eyes and released Bobby. "Yeah. Bobby needs our help to get his boat up and ready."

Kent's forehead furrowed. "Trouble with Brad again?"

"Again? Try always." Bobby shook his head. "I'm just not happy. I think I need to make a break, and getting *My Second Chance* finished would give me another job and place to live."

Kent set the case of beer on the counter. "I'll be more than happy to do what I can, but I've got a feeling the real problem might just follow you."

"I'm not in the mood to be psychoanalysed." Kent was a good guy, but he had way too many opinions on other peoples' problems, especially because the guy needed to take care of his own first.

"Just trying to help," Kent mumbled, opening a beer.

"Since when?" Marco asked, coming into the room.

"Fuck you, De Le Santo," Kent huffed and disappeared into the living room.

Zac put his hands on his hips and regarded Marco. "Be nice, please?"

Marco grinned and blew Zac a kiss. "For you, I'll be a good boy."

The innocent look on Marco's face dispelled Bobby's dour mood. His friends always had a way of making him feel better. He heard the front door open and Trey and Angelo's voices as they greeted Kent.

He clapped his hands and briskly rubbed them together. "So, who's ready to give me their money?"

* * * *

Standing on the porch, Bobby had his thumbs hooked into his jeans pockets when his father opened the door. "Hi, Dad."

His dad seemed to scrutinise Bobby's appearance before stepping back into the foyer. "Afternoon, Robert."

Bobby gave an inward sigh at the loving endearment. He'd gone by Bobby since he was old enough to have a say in the matter, but his uptight father still refused to call him anything other than his given name.

"Where's Mom?"

"Your mother is in the sunroom with the rest of the family."

Bobby quickly wondered if it was too late to escape. He should've declined the dinner and asked his mom to meet him somewhere instead.

His dad led the way to the rest of the group. When Bobby didn't immediately follow, Joseph turned and cleared his throat.

"Yeah, I'm coming." Bobby followed after his dad, the tension already building in his neck and shoulders. He braced himself for the upcoming meeting as if he were headed for battle.

The back right corner of the house was a huge room with glass on two sides, various tropical plants and flowers growing in raised stone beds. Bobby stopped by his mother's chair and placed a dutiful kiss on her upturned cheek. "Hey, Mom."

"Good to see you, Son," his mother said, smiling up at him. "Have you lost weight?"

Bobby rubbed his flat stomach. "Nope, not that I know of. I haven't had a chance to get much sun yet this season, which usually makes a difference."

"Too much time in the sun isn't healthy," his mom reminded him.

"I know." Bobby took one of the available rattan chairs and sat down. His two nephews, ages three and five stood by their mother's side staring.

It was a shame he wasn't closer to the two small boys. He had nothing at all against children, but he still hadn't decided what species to put Alexander and Ralston in. Seriously, who the hell names a child Ralston besides someone as pretentious as Brad?

"Hi, Olivia, boys."

"Did you get the fax I sent?" Brad asked in lieu of a greeting.

"Uh, no, when did you send it?" Bobby asked.

"Late last night. Don't you check your machine? You know, the reason I bought it…"

"I was playing poker with my friends, give me a break. I'll look at it when I get back."

Brad huffed and glanced at his father. "This is the reason we aren't making the money we should."

Bobby felt like he'd been punched in the stomach. "We?" He turned to his dad. "You own part of *The Gypsy*?"

Joseph blustered around for a few seconds before answering. "Yes. We thought it best that you didn't know."

Taking a deep breath, Bobby rose and regarded his mother. "I'll call you later, Mom."

He barely made it to his Jeep before his eyes filled with tears. It was one thing to have his half-brother go behind his back and take his dream, but his own father?

Starting the Jeep, Bobby peeled out of the driveway. One thing was certain, he was finished working and living on *The Gypsy*. His dad and Brad had completely destroyed every good thing about his old boat.

It didn't take long for Bobby to gather his clothes and dishes and load them into the Jeep. He pulled out his phone and called Kent, the only friend he knew with a truck.

"Hello," Kent answered.

"It's Bobby. Are you busy today?"

"Not really, why?"

"I'm moving my stuff out of *The Gypsy* and could use your truck."

"Whoa, that's a pretty big step."

"Yeah, well it's been a long time coming. So, can I borrow your truck?"

"I'll be there as soon as I can."

While waiting for Kent, Bobby fired up his laptop and drafted a formal letter of resignation. It would be just like Brad to try and weasel out of paying him severance. He also used the opportunity to check his savings account balance.

Bobby was busy trying to make out a budget for himself when he heard a familiar voice call his name. He stood and glanced over the side of the boat.

"Permission to come aboard?" Jules called up.

Bobby's gut clenched at the handsome older man. "Sure."

He shut down the laptop before turning to face Jules. "If you've come to reschedule your cruise, I'm sorry I can't help you. I just quit."

Jules shook his head. "Actually, I came to apologise for my actions the last time we saw each other."

"Oh." Bobby stuffed the laptop into its case. "No reason to apologise. We both let things get out of hand."

Jules shoved his hands in his pockets. "Well, I guess that's one way of looking at it. I was thinking more along the lines that I shouldn't have pushed you away like I did."

Bobby nearly dropped the box of books he'd bent to pick up. "What?"

Jules' face had a distinct red hue to it. "I came by to see if you'd be interested in going out to dinner with me?"

Bobby ran a hand through his short dark hair. A large part of him wanted to accept the invitation, but he had other problems on his mind. "Sorry, I can't. As you can see I'm moving."

Jules took in the boxes surrounding Bobby. "Can I help?"

Chapter Four

After getting the boxes unloaded from Kent's truck, Bobby took off to buy a mattress. While he was gone, Jules and Kent attempted to clean as much of the salon as they could. Three trash bags later, Jules collapsed in the cracked leather chair.

"Should we try putting away the dishes?" he asked Kent.

Kent scratched his jaw and shook his head. "I don't see any other choice. If we don't get these boxes outta here, there won't be room to move, let alone try to live."

Kent carried one of the boxes to the small galley. "I hate this."

"What?" Jules asked, setting a box on the tiny stove.

"Seeing Bobby try to live in this shithole. It just ain't right. He worked his ass off on *The Gypsy*. That's where he should be, not here. This boat will never make him happy."

Jules looked around the interior. "You're in construction, right?"

"Yeah."

"Know anyone who could help Bobby make this place the showpiece it used to be?"

"Sure, but Bobby can't pay for it and he won't take favours like that."

Jules put his mind to work, trying like hell to come up with a solution. "He'll need a job, right?"

"Yeah. He's worked for me before. I'm sure I can find something for him to do."

"Maybe you could convince him to barter with you for the things he needs done." Jules hated to stick his nose into Bobby's business, but he didn't know how the man was going to live on a boat with no running water and only an extension cord from one of Kent's outbuildings for power.

Kent nodded. "I'll try to work it into the conversation. One thing you need to learn about Bobby is the man can be stubborn as a mule. If he thinks I'm doing him a favour, he'll never go for it."

Jules filed the information away for later use.

"Can one of you guys help me carry this aboard?" Bobby called out.

Kent grinned and nudged Jules with his elbow. "The damn television almost killed me trying to get it up here. I think the mattress will take all three of us."

Jules nodded, eager to help. So far, Bobby seemed to be treating him with kid gloves, only handing Jules the lighter boxes to carry up. Jules knew he didn't have near the muscle mass Bobby had, but he wasn't a wimp.

* * * *

By the time they wrestled the full-size mattress into the captain's cabin, sweat was running down Bobby's face. He pulled the dripping T-shirt over his head and wiped his face, chest and underarms before tossing it aside.

When he looked up, he caught Jules staring at him. Fuck. The look in the older man's eyes had Bobby's cock hard as stone in seconds. He turned his back to the berth, and began fidgeting with the bed.

"I think I'll go ahead and make this while I'm here. Why don't you guys grab a couple of beers and relax." Bobby dug a set of sheets out of the trash bag he'd brought stuff over in and turned to make the bed.

Jules stood right in front of him, close enough to touch. "I'll help."

Bobby swallowed around the lump in his throat. Need raced through his body as he stared into the blue depths of Jules' eyes. The older man reached out first, running a hand down the centre of Bobby's chest, only to travel back up again.

Why would a man who had everything want him? Bobby tried to figure it out as he allowed the soft caress. "Are you feeling sorry for me?"

Jules took a step closer until their bodies were pressed together. "I'm feeling something, but sorry isn't the right word for it."

Bobby felt the proof of Jules' arousal rub against his own hard cock.

"Hey, you guys want one?" Kent asked, coming in with a couple of beers. "Oh, sorry."

Jules gave Bobby a wistful smile and stepped back. "I'll take one."

Bobby could tell Kent was suddenly uncomfortable with the situation, so decided to save his friend from further embarrassment. "I'm finished with the truck."

"Okay, great. Well then I think I'll take off. Call me later?" Kent asked, sliding towards the door.

"Yeah. As you can imagine, I'm gonna need to find a job in the morning."

"Not a problem. Let me go over my work logs and see what I can come up with."

Bobby stepped forward and placed a hand on Kent's shoulder. His friend may have his faults, but he'd always been there when Bobby had needed him. "Thanks. For everything," he added.

"No need," Kent said and shook Jules' hand. "It was nice to see you again."

"Same here," Jules returned.

Kent left and Bobby stood alone in the small cabin with the sexiest man he'd ever known. "Hungry? I could pay you back for all your help with dinner?"

Damn. Listen to him. Bobby knew he sounded like a scared virgin, but the attraction to Jules was too strong to trust it.

Jules flashed him a knowing grin. "Dinner sounds nice."

* * * *

They ended up downtown at a little hole in the wall Jules favoured. "Nothing fancy, but they have the best food in town."

"Sounds good to me," Bobby answered, sliding into one of the booths.

The place looked more like a beer joint than anything else, but good food was good food. "What do you recommend?"

Jules didn't even open his menu. "Whatever's on special. I've never had anything I didn't like here."

The waitress stepped up to the table. "What can I get you?"

Winking at Bobby, Jules smiled at the waitress. "What's the special?"

"Meatloaf, mashed potatoes and green beans, salad to start."

"That sounds good, and bring me a glass of ice water, please."

"I'll have the same," Bobby agreed with Jules' choice.

The waitress nodded and walked off, leaving the two of them alone. Bobby tapped his fingers idly on the table, his mind and body a jumble of nerves.

Jules' hand covered his and Bobby automatically turned his over to thread their fingers together.

"What's wrong?" Jules asked.

"I don't know. I guess I'm a little nervous," he admitted.

Bobby moved to cup Jules' hand between the two of his. The doctor's hand was so different from his own long fingers, spotless nails. "So soft."

"Is that what's bothering you?"

Surprised at how close the observation hit home, Bobby released Jules' hand.

"What I do for a living has nothing to do with us."

Although he knew it was unfair, thoughts of his father's and brother's betrayal assaulted him once again. "You're wrong."

He stared Jules in the eyes. "Someone like me will never be able to make you happy."

Instead of getting angry, Jules did the unexpected. He stood and slid in next to Bobby. Without saying a word, he wrapped his arm around Bobby's back and kissed him.

"Who is it that's made you feel inferior?" he whispered in Bobby's ear.

Bobby shook his head. "I don't feel inferior. I don't know where you got that idea. I just know I can't fit into your world. I've tried before and it didn't work."

"My world is a big house and old cars. I have acquaintances, not friends. My parents are gone. So tell me, what won't you fit into?" Jules asked, punctuating each sentence with a kiss to Bobby's neck.

God help him but it felt good. Bobby tilted his head to the side to give Jules more room. The waitress cleared her throat as she set their plates in front of them. Jules nipped Bobby's neck before releasing his hold.

"Thank you," Jules told the waitress.

She gave them an uneasy nod before walking away.

Bobby gazed down at his food. It looked wonderful, so why wasn't he eating? Jules' hand landed on his thigh.

"It's good, eat up."

* * * *

"You wanna come up?" Bobby asked.

As much as Jules wanted to do just that, he shook his head. "I think slow and easy is the way to win this race. I have to work this week, but what're you doing Friday night?"

"Nothin', just working on the boat. You wanna come by?" Bobby asked.

"I'd like that. Can I bring dinner?"

Bobby nodded. "Anything but sushi, that shit's nasty."

Jules chuckled. "I'll remember that."

He leaned over and gave Bobby a goodnight kiss. As he delved his tongue inside, Bobby moaned, threatening to undo all Jules' good intentions. Pulling back he licked his lips. "I need to go."

Bobby started to say something, but snapped his mouth shut and nodded. "Okay, Friday then."

"Can I call you?" Jules asked.

Bobby smiled and withdrew a card from his wallet. "The rest of the stuff on here isn't accurate anymore, but the cell phone's still mine."

Jules took the card and pulled out one of his own. "I'm hit or miss during the day, but if you get a chance, call me."

Bobby took the card and ran the edge over his swollen lips. Jules knew the man wasn't even aware of the power of his actions, but drawing attention to that gorgeous mouth was almost his undoing. He found himself leaning towards those lips once again.

Bobby's hand shot out, stopping him. "If you kiss me again, I'm not gonna let you leave."

Jules laughed. "Fair enough."

He watched Bobby get out of the car and climb the makeshift ladder to the deck of the boat. With a wave,

Jules started his car and drove towards the guard's station. Instead of pulling right through when the gate opened, Jules slowed the car to a stop beside the man on duty.

"Just thought I'd introduce myself since you'll be seeing a lot of me in the future."

* * * *

Jules was suturing a leg wound, when Eric came skidding into the curtained off exam room.

"Critical coming in, can I get your help?" Eric asked.

"I'll be there in a second," Jules replied calmly as he tied the last knot.

He stepped back from the young boy and shook his finger. "No more jumping off the roof, you hear me?"

The boy nodded as his mother gathered their things. "The nurse will be in with wound care and follow-up instructions."

"Thank you, Dr. Peters. I can't believe Grant did something so stupid," the boy's mother admonished.

Jules grinned. "All part of growing up."

He removed his latex gloves and tossed them into the hazardous waste bin, before rushing to help Eric.

He found Eric inserting an intubation tube into a patient's throat. Reaching into the box on the wall, Jules extracted another pair of gloves. "What've you got?"

"RTA, crushed chest cavity, collapsed lungs, multiple fractures to right tib and fib and the humerus in both arms," Eric recited as he concentrated on his patient.

Stepping up to the gurney, Jules felt the room begin to spin. He reached out and tried to steady himself, but lost the battle when his world went black.

"Dr. Peters?"

Jules could hear a voice, but couldn't get his damn eyelids to cooperate. "Yeah?"

"Sir, you passed out. Can you open your eyes?"

After a few moments, Jules managed to do as asked. He was lying on a gurney in the ER. "What…what happened?"

"I don't know. You went in to help Dr. Stanton with a patient, took one look at him and fainted. You hit your head on the bottom of the bed."

Jules remembered looking down into a face that eerily resembled Morgan's. The patient could've been his deceased lover's twin. He started to lift his hand towards his face, but Dr. Braverman stilled it. "Dr. Peters, you need stitches."

Jules nodded his consent, the movement sending shards of pain through his skull.

"Would you like me to call someone?" Braverman asked.

"There is no one," Jules mumbled. The thought of Bobby by his side flashed into his head, but Jules pushed it away, the image of Morgan in the seconds before death still fresh in his mind.

As Braverman began to suture his head wound, Jules closed his eyes. He remembered the last words his beloved had spoken to him. "Please help me."

After all the years of putting medicine before his relationship, he couldn't do the one thing Morgan had asked, too many injuries, too little time. He'd watched the man he loved die in front of him, and could do nothing to stop it.

"I love you," he'd whispered.

Morgan's eyes filled with tears as the life drained from his body. Jules had never been able to overcome that look. It wasn't love he saw in Morgan's eyes, it was disappointment.

Yelling in the hallway snapped Jules out of the past.

"Someone had better tell me something. All I know is Dr. Peters has been injured. Now where is he?"

Jules took a deep breath. Bobby's boisterous voice shouldn't be able to bring him so much peace, so why did it? Jules licked his dry lips.

"Would you please bring him in here so he won't wake everyone in the damn hospital?" he asked Braverman.

Chuckling, the young doctor stuck his head out the door. "Dr. Peters is in here."

Jules heard shuffling, seconds before Bobby towered over him.

"What happened?" Bobby asked, his eyes full of concern.

"I'm fine. Just fainted and bumped my head."

Bobby grabbed his chest. "Damn. When I got the call they didn't give me any details. Scared the shit out of me."

"Eric?"

Bobby shook his head. "No. Some lady who said Eric asked her to call."

Jules made a mental note to speak with Eric about meddling in his business. "I'm fine, really."

As Bobby continued to stare down at him, Dr. Braverman finished his suturing and placed a bandage over the wound. "I'd suggest you go home for the rest of the day. Other than that, you know the drill."

Jules nodded. "Thanks."

Braverman left and Jules reached out a hand. "Can you help me up?"

Instead of grabbing Jules' hand, Bobby slid an arm under his back and lifted him into a sitting position. "Come on, I'll drive ya home."

Jules started to argue, but stopped himself. "I'd appreciate it."

"Do I need to get a wheelchair?" Bobby asked.

"No, I should be fine to walk."

Bobby helped Jules down from the bed and hugged him. "I'm glad you're okay."

The whispered words against his ear warmed Jules to his toes. He wrapped his arms around Bobby and returned the embrace. Though his sexual preference wasn't advertised at work, Jules wasn't about to push the man away because of what his colleagues might think.

"If you'll pull your car around, I'll get my briefcase and meet you out front," he said, placing a soft kiss on Bobby's cheek.

Bobby stepped back, his beautiful brown eyes straying to the bandage on Jules' forehead. "Sure you're okay to walk?"

"I'm fine. I see real-life emergencies every day, believe me, this is nothing."

Bobby nodded and disappeared down the hall. Jules headed towards the lounge, almost running into Eric as he turned a corner. "Dr. Stanton."

Eric's eyes went wide. "Please don't be mad at me. I knew you wouldn't be able to drive home, and I hoped things between you and Bobby had progressed enough that I could have him called down here for you."

It said much about the smaller man's character that Jules couldn't stay mad at him. Although he'd planned to give Eric a piece of his mind, he ended up smiling. "Actually, I wanted to thank you."

"Really?"

"Yes, really, but don't let it happen again," Jules added with a shake of his finger.

"Yes, sir, Dr. Peters, sir." Eric finished it off with an exaggerated salute.

"Smart ass," Jules chuckled as he continued to the lounge.

He retrieved his briefcase and signed himself out, promising himself that he'd fill out an accident report in the morning. Bobby must have been waiting for him, because the second Jules stepped out of the hospital, the younger man pulled up in front of him.

Jules climbed up into the old green Jeep and set his briefcase at his feet. The movement caused a moment of dizziness, and Jules blinked several times, trying to right his world.

"You okay?" Bobby asked, hand on Jules' back.

"Yeah, shouldn't have bent over so fast," he answered, putting a hand on Bobby's thigh to reassure him.

Bobby pulled out of the parking lot and turned towards Jules' house. On the way, they drove past one of the more exclusive neighbourhoods.

"That's where I grew up," Bobby mumbled in an off-hand manner.

Jules kept his shock hidden. He'd understood from Eric that Bobby's brother had money, but no one had clued Jules in that the man grew up with it. He wondered what part of Bobby's childhood played in his distrust for people with money?

"Where should I park?" Bobby asked when they pulled into Jules' drive.

"Anywhere's fine."

Bobby parked in front of the house and turned off the engine. "Hold on."

He got out and came around to Jules' side. Reaching out, Bobby helped Jules down from the Jeep. Bobby must've seen the protest forming on Jules' lips. "Indulge me, will ya?"

Jules rolled his eyes and let Bobby lead him. He dug out his keys and unlocked the door. As soon as they were both inside, Jules punched his security code into the alarm system on the wall.

"Where's your bedroom?" Bobby asked.

"Upstairs at the end of the hall." He felt stupid letting Bobby baby him, but after years of living alone, it was too good to turn down.

Entering the master suite, Jules pulled off his bloodied shirt. He watched Bobby's ass as the gorgeous man turned down the sheets. "I don't really think going to bed is necessary."

Bobby reached down and pulled off his own T-shirt. "Yes it is."

Chapter Five

Sitting on the side of the bed, Bobby reached out and pulled Jules forward by the waist of his pants. Without saying a word, Bobby began rubbing his face against Jules' bare chest, snaking his tongue out for an occasional lick.

Jules buried his fingers in Bobby's thick dark hair and tilted his head back. "Yeah, right there," he moaned as Bobby's tongue began flicking and circling his nipples.

While Bobby's mouth was busy torturing him, his hands were going in for the kill, kneading his burgeoning erection through the material that separated them. Jules wanted to strip naked and present his ass to the man, but he knew they needed to relish this first time together.

Teeth scraped against his chest as Bobby unfastened Jules' pants. Once unzipped, the material fell around

Jules' ankles. Bobby worked his way down Jules' torso to the bulge straining the front of his boxer-briefs.

Jules' breath hitched as Bobby began to mouth the front of his underwear. Jules tilted Bobby's chin up. "Take them off."

Bobby grinned, flashing those million dollar dimples. "I thought you'd never ask."

The saturated briefs were pulled down and Jules took a step, kicking his pants and underwear aside. Jules put his hands on Bobby's shoulders and gave him a gentle push.

Bobby lay back on the bed, his feet still firmly planted on the floor, as Jules climbed over the top of him. Sitting on Bobby's upper chest, Jules touched the head of his cock to his lover's lips.

With a groan, Bobby licked the pre-cum from Jules' crown before sliding his lips down the shaft.

Once inside Bobby's mouth, Jules couldn't hold back. His hips started a slow shallow thrust as he fucked Bobby's throat. For his part, Bobby was a fantastic cock sucker. Jules couldn't remember a blowjob ever feeling so good. It may have had something to do with going without for so long, but he doubted it.

Bobby's hands slid from Jules' hips down to cup his ass. Spreading the cheeks apart, Bobby's finger began a seductive dance across Jules' hole. *Yes, fuck me.* Damn, had he ever wanted someone like he wanted Bobby at that moment?

Pulling his cock free of Bobby's mouth, Jules looked down into the younger man's eyes. "I need you inside me."

Bobby licked his swollen lips and nodded. "You have stuff?"

Did he? Jules mentally inventoried his bedside drawer and medicine cabinet. He seemed to remember...

"Yes," he shouted in glee and jumped off the bed. Jules opened the cabinet under the sink in his en suite and rummaged around. He'd attended a medical conference the previous year and had received a new brand of condoms in his introductory bag. When he got home he almost threw them out, but tossed them into the cabinet just in case. Damn, he was glad he did.

With the box of three condoms in hand, Jules moved back to the bed, holding the box aloft in triumph. "I knew I had some somewhere."

He handed a gloriously naked Bobby the box and dug his bottle of lube from the bedside drawer. No need to go searching for that. He'd used the slick nightly since first laying eyes on Bobby Quinn.

Bobby started laughing, as he rolled the condom down his thick length.

Jules' mouth dropped open at the vibrant pink and green striped latex. The prominent veins in Bobby's cock, combined with the vertical stripes, made Jules dizzy.

"They're from a convention," he said by way of explanation.

Still laughing, Bobby pinched the reservoir tip to give himself extra room. "Evidently they didn't go over well, because I've never seen anything like them."

Jules smiled and handed the well-used bottle to the laughing man. Crawling to the centre of the king-sized bed, Jules remained on his hands and knees and glanced over his shoulder. Bobby had added a couple of drops of the slick to his cock and was slowly stroking up and down its length.

Jules wasn't the kind of man to be shy in the bedroom, so he wiggled his ass several times. "Come and get it."

Shaking his head, Bobby's chuckles died as his eyes zeroed in on Jules' butt. With another lick of his lips, Bobby took his place behind Jules.

"Mmm," Bobby moaned, taking his first taste of Jules' hole.

Jules' hands fisted the sheet under him. He spread his legs further apart as Bobby's tongue began to probe his sphincter. "Fuck me."

Jules heard the click of the lube cap seconds before a slick finger was introduced. Bobby expertly stretched him, whispering words full of lustful intentions.

"Gonna make you feel so good, you never forget me."

Squeezing his eyes shut, Jules nodded. He already knew he'd never forget Bobby Quinn, the fucking had nothing to do with it. Jules grinned, although it was definitely an added bonus. "I'm ready."

Biting the cheek of Jules' ass, Bobby removed his fingers and replaced them with the head of his brightly coloured cock. With the thick length of his lover's erection slowly filling him, Jules laid his head on the pillow, leaving his ass in the air.

A picture of a man with shoulder-length blond hair came to mind as Bobby's cock was fully seated in his ass.

"Damn, you feel good."

Jules' eyes shot open at the low, rugged voice. *Fuck. Bobby.* Jules groaned as shame overtook him. How in the world could he have forgotten it was Bobby in his bed and not Morgan? Jules wanted to run from the room. He didn't deserve a man like Bobby.

"Am I hurting you?" Bobby asked. "You're tense all of a sudden."

Jules closed his eyes again, trying to get his emotions under control. "Can...will you make love to me face to face?"

Bobby's body stilled behind him. "Something wrong?"

Jules peered over his shoulder. "I just need to see your face."

He vowed to never tell Bobby what had just happened. It wasn't that he wasn't developing feelings for his new lover, but Morgan had been the only one to fuck him. With Morgan, Jules had been strictly a bottom. After his partner's death, the few times he'd hooked up with someone, he'd made it clear up front that he topped only. So what was different? Why was he allowing Bobby a gift he'd only given to one other man?

Bobby pulled out, and Jules rolled over. He hoped Bobby wouldn't notice the shame he still felt at the mistake. He reached up and ran his fingers through Bobby's dark hair. The man was so gorgeous and looked nothing like Morgan. Yes, face to face was much better.

He wrapped his long legs around Bobby's waist, suddenly needing the man as close as possible. Without breaking eye contact, Bobby repositioned his cock to Jules' entrance. The forward thrust of Bobby's hips filled Jules with a totally different sensation. It was no longer a simple fuck, and the realisation scared him.

"Yessss," Bobby hissed, starting a slow rhythm.

Jules pulled Bobby's head down for a kiss. *Forgive me, Morgan.* In the few short days since they'd met, Bobby was quickly becoming the most important person in Jules' life. The carefully arranged photographs on the dresser caught his eye. Morgan's blue eyes stared at him from his graduation photo. Jules looked at each photograph lining the dresser. The fishing trip the two of them had taken, the rowdy frat party pictures, they were all there in living colour. Would he be able to put Morgan to rest after all these years?

"Are you with me?" Bobby growled.

Jules' gaze darted away from the pictures and back to Bobby. "Sorry."

Bobby pulled out of Jules' ass and swung his legs over the side of the bed. Looking around the room, he seemed to settle on the photographs of Jules and Morgan. "Is that your boyfriend that died?"

Jules cleared his throat. "Yes."

Had he ever felt so humiliated? To be so obviously caught looking at pictures of another man while being fucked. He wanted to tell Bobby he didn't need to worry, that he'd just been considering putting the pictures away.

Before he had a chance to explain, Bobby stood and walked over to the dresser. Jules couldn't help but to stare at Bobby's muscled ass as he picked up each individual frame.

Climbing off the bed, Jules wrapped his arms around his lover's waist. "I need to put them away. I'm sorry."

Bobby set the sterling silver frame back in its place. Jules began peppering kisses to Bobby's broad back. *Please forgive me?*

"I won't compete against a dead guy," Bobby mumbled without turning around.

"No, of course not." Jules went around and slithered in between Bobby and the photographs.

"I've never had a reason to put them away." He placed a soft kiss on Bobby's lips. "Until now."

Bobby eventually wrapped his arms around Jules. "Why don't you try and get some rest. I'll run out and get us something to eat."

So much for making love. "I'm sorry."

Bobby shook his head. "You like pizza or burgers better?"

"Either," Jules mumbled.

Bobby nodded and picked his discarded clothes up before retreating to the bathroom. Jules turned and studied the photographs. Most of them were him and Morgan at various frat house functions before Jules had entered med school. *Of course they were, because I didn't make much time for Morgan after those first four years.*

He heard the door open and spun away from the painful memories. Bobby was fully dressed and looking like he wanted to be anywhere but where he was. "You're coming back, right?"

Bobby sighed and stepped up to Jules. "I can't lie and say what happened a few minutes ago didn't hurt, but I'm trying to understand."

"I'll put them away while you're gone," Jules promised.

Bobby shook his head. "It's not the pictures, Jules. Until you can get beyond his death, putting frames in a drawer isn't going to help."

"I know. It's just…Morgan's the only man who's ever made love to me. I guess having you inside me must've triggered something."

Jules reached out and cupped Bobby's cheek. "You're the first person to stir up these long dormant feelings. I'd very much like to see where they lead us."

Bobby turned his head and placed a kiss on Jules' palm. "I'd like that."

* * * *

Pulling into Burger Max, Bobby picked up his phone and punched in Zac's number.

"Hello."

"It's me. Is Eric home yet?"

"No, he's working until seven, why?"

"I need to talk to him about Jules. See if he knows anything about his ex-boyfriend."

"The one who died?" Zac asked.

"Yeah."

"Well I don't know a lot, but I know Dr. Peters and his partner were together a long time. They must've been pretty young though because the guy died two years after Jules became a doctor."

Bobby wasn't sure exactly how old Jules was, but he'd guess early to mid-forties. "That's gotta be close to eighteen, nineteen years ago."

"Probably pretty damn close," Zac agreed.

195

Had Jules been in mourning all those years? From what he'd said in the bedroom earlier, Bobby's guess was yes. How was he supposed to vanquish a twenty-year old ghost?

"Thanks. I'll talk to you later," he finally said.

"Bobby? Is there anything I can do?"

"No. It's pretty much all on us at this point." He said his goodbyes and shoved the phone back into his pocket.

No sooner had he pulled up to the drive-thru speaker than his phone started ringing. He saw from the display it was Kent. "Hey, can you hang on a sec?"

"Sure."

"Can I help you?"

"Yeah, give me four double cheeseburgers, two large fries, two large onion rings and two chocolate shakes."

"Okay, I'm back," he told Kent as he pulled around to the window and dug out his wallet.

"How's Jules?"

"Okay, I think. He's resting at his place. I just ran out to pick us up something to eat."

"That's good. Listen, I've got a job for you if you want it. Nothing fancy, just site clean-up and errand guy, but it's yours if you're interested."

Bobby squeezed his eyes shut. He hated clean-up detail. He'd done it before and knew exactly how much sweat was involved. He handed a twenty through the window. "Sure, sounds good."

"Good." Kent gave him the location of the construction site. At least it wasn't far from where he had his boat dry-docked. "Be there by seven-thirty."

"Tonight?" Bobby asked, taking his food from the pimply faced kid.

"No, jackass, in the morning."

"Yeah, of course, sorry."

"Don't be late," Kent reminded him. Everyone who worked for Kent knew he was a stickler when it came to showing up on time. The only one who ever dared defy the big boss man was Marco, and Bobby thought it was only to get Kent's attention.

"You gonna be home later?" Kent asked.

Would he? "The jury's still out on that, why?"

"I have some wood flooring left over from a job. Thought I'd see if it's enough to put in your boat. If it is, I was kinda hoping you'd buy it from me. I'll give it to you for a steal."

"Does it have to be tonight?"

"No, no hurry."

He pulled into Jules' drive. "I'll give you a call if I don't see you at the site."

"Okay, see ya."

Bobby grabbed the bags, and walked towards the house. He stood in front of the door for several moments. Was he supposed to go inside without knocking? What if the alarm was on? *Shit.* Bobby gave up and rang the bell.

The door opened and Jules smiled. "You came back."

Bobby didn't miss the red-rimmed eyes in front of him. "Of course I did."

As Jules led him into the kitchen, Bobby couldn't help but wonder who Jules had been crying over. Had he once again mourned his dead lover, or did he truly think Bobby wouldn't return? Could the idea of not seeing him again upset the man to the point of tears?

Jules sat at the kitchen table and Bobby laid the food out in front of him. "Wasn't sure how hungry you'd be, so I got extra just in case."

Jules' eyes popped wide open at the array of fast food. "I should say."

"Mind if I get some ketchup?" Bobby asked.

"Uh, no, not at all. Door of the fridge." Jules opened one of the cheeseburgers and stared at it.

Bobby shook his head and went to the fridge. He found the ketchup immediately, but also spotted a bottle of steak sauce. Taking both back to the table, he wasn't surprised to find Jules still staring at his food. "Eat up."

Jules jumped a little and picked up his burger. Bobby flattened out the paper his burger had come in and poured two big piles of thick dippings on it. He noticed Jules looking at him funny. "What? Steak sauce is better with fries, but you gotta have ketchup for onion rings."

Jules gifted him with a half grin. "I'll have to try it."

Bobby finished the first burger in no time and started on the second. He glanced at Jules. The man had barely eaten a quarter of his. "You don't like 'em?"

It was obvious Jules was trying to think up an excuse, but he finally set his food on the table. "Sorry, guess I'm not hungry."

This was the part of a relationship Bobby sucked at, and he knew it. Did he pull whatever was bothering Jules out of him, or wait for Jules to come to him? What if Jules had decided he didn't want anyone besides Morgan? Although the idea made Bobby sick to his stomach, he needed to know if he was wasting his time.

He ate the second burger and started in on the fries. He'd always been the kind of person to completely finish one food before starting on the next. "So, did you get any rest while I was gone?"

Jules shook his head, still staring down at his partially eaten dinner. "No. I put Morgan's things away. I know you told me it wouldn't help, but I needed to start somewhere."

Jules sighed and rubbed his eyes. "I don't know why I let myself live in such a cocoon for so long."

Standing, Jules took his barely eaten sandwich to the trash. "You know, it's not just about Morgan being everywhere in this house. I doubt that you noticed, but this place is filled with pictures of dead people. This house belonged to my sister, Beth. She inherited it from my Aunt Ida."

Jules turned and stuck his hands in his pockets, gazing out the big window. "Beth died of leukaemia eight years ago. Now there's just me. I guess I had the pictures up more out of loneliness than anything else."

Bobby stood and walked over to Jules. Wrapping his arms around the man he was quickly beginning to truly care about, he hugged him. Not sure of what to say, he remained silent and offered support the best way he knew.

Sure, his own family sucked, but at least he had his friends. Bobby didn't think Jules even had that. What he couldn't figure out was why. Was it by choice, or design?

It was another week and a half before the next poker night, and Bobby didn't want to wait that long. "I was thinking of having a get-together on the boat Saturday. Nothing fancy, just burgers, dogs and beer. The guys are coming over to help me work on the hull. Wanna come?"

Jules reached up and crossed his arms over Bobby's. "I'll have to check my schedule, but yeah, I'd like that."

"Cool, it's a date." Bobby kissed Jules' neck, inhaling the subtle hint of whatever designer cologne his lover wore. "Feel like watching some TV?"

* * * *

Spooned on the sofa in front of Bobby, Jules tried to concentrate on the survival show his lover had turned on.

Bobby's hand rested under Jules' shirt, idly rubbing circles against Jules' skin. Had he ever just sat and watched television with a lover? He knew he and Morgan had never done it. Between studying and his work at the hospital, Jules was lucky to spend any time at all with his partner. A good day for them was several stolen hours in bed.

Jules snuggled even further against Bobby. The more he thought about it, the more he realised his life with Morgan was either about sex or work. Did they even talk much towards the end? He didn't blame either of them anymore. Jules' passion for medicine didn't always jive with Morgan's passion for goofing off, but he liked to think they were relatively happy in their relationship.

"I love this guy," Bobby commented, when the hot little stud on TV began to eat a raw fish.

"Ooh, why do you like this show?" he asked.

Bobby's hand wandered further up Jules' chest. "I don't know. I guess because it's a show about taking what you're given and making the most of it."

Jules pressed his ass against Bobby's crotch. "Are you sure it has nothing to do with the fact he's sex on a stick?"

Bobby chuckled and reached up to pinch Jules' nipple. "Oh, that doesn't hurt, but it's really not the reason I watch."

Jules trapped Bobby's hand where it was, the delicious sensation of his lover's fingers torturing his nipple too good to give up. He felt his cock fill, tenting out the fabric of his navy pyjama pants.

"Oh, you like that, do you?" Bobby teased, nipping Jules' earlobe.

Jules started to roll over, but Bobby stopped him. "Just stay where you are and let me love you."

Stilling, Jules' brow crinkled, making him wince when the stitches pulled against his flesh. "You don't want me to reciprocate?"

Bobby's hand travelled down Jules' stomach to the elastic band of his pyjama bottoms. "This is for you. I just want to lie here and touch every inch of your body."

"What about you?" Jules asked as Bobby's hand slipped down the front of his pants.

Encircling Jules' cock in his hand, Bobby pressed the hard ridge of his erection against Jules' ass. "Don't worry about me. I'm doing just fine."

Jules decided to give himself over to Bobby's brand of loving. The hand on his cock felt divine as he settled into his lover's comforting embrace.

"I noticed you took down all the pictures in this room," Bobby whispered, pressing his thumb to the underside of Jules' cockhead.

Jules nodded. "Like I told you, it wasn't just photographs of Morgan that were making this place more like a mausoleum than a home."

Bobby released Jules' erection and started pushing his pants down. Jules lifted his hip off the sofa and kicked them off. Bobby groaned and positioned Jules' left leg atop his own, opening Jules further.

"I think you should put some of them back. There's nothing wrong with having memories around you. As long as you don't use them to replace the present and the future, there's nothing wrong with it."

Is that what he'd done? Jules nodded to himself. That's exactly what he'd done. "Maybe some of my parents and sister, but I think I'll leave Morgan packed away, at least for now."

Bobby's hands massaged Jules' balls as he licked the side of Jules' neck. "Although I'm trying to take Morgan's place in your bed, I'm not stupid enough to think I'll ever get him out of your heart."

With Bobby's finger brushing against his hole, Jules didn't want to analyse his feelings for Morgan. Instead of answering, he reached back and lifted Bobby's hand to his mouth. Laving the callused digits, he applied as much spit as he could.

"You needing, babe?" Bobby asked, removing his fingers and moving them back to Jules' hole.

Jules nodded. "Please."

Chuckling, Bobby inserted the tip of his middle finger, stopping at the first knuckle. "Is this what you want?"

Jules pushed back, impaling himself. "More."

Slowly fucking Jules with his finger, Bobby moaned. "I don't know about you, but I need a little more."

Bobby wiggled out from behind Jules and flipped him onto his back. Placing one of Jules' legs over the back of the sofa, Bobby smiled. "You're so fucking hot like this, open to my eyes, fingers and tongue."

To prove it, Bobby manoeuvred himself between Jules' spread thighs and inhaled. Bobby spat and warm saliva ran down the crack of Jules' ass. As Bobby nuzzled and licked Jules' balls, his fingers were busy sawing in and out of his hole.

Jules couldn't remember ever feeling so completely stimulated. It was hard to breathe. He gasped as Bobby's mouth sunk down on his cock. "Shit," Jules panted.

He could hear a zipper lower and knew Bobby was shucking his jeans. "Fuck me."

Bobby released Jules' shaft and shook his head. "Nope, I already said this was all about you."

"Yes, and I want you to fuck me," he begged.

Bobby winked. "Plenty of time for that later. Just relax and ride it out."

Ride it out? Hell, Jules' cock was about to explode into a million pieces. The scrape of Bobby's teeth as he sucked Jules' length down his throat, was enough to push him over the edge.

Gripping handfuls of Bobby's hair, Jules yelled out his climax. "Coming!"

He bit his lip as he pumped his seed down Bobby's throat.

Still nursing Jules' cock, Bobby groaned as his body began to buck and vibrate with his own release.

The two of them laid on the sofa like a couple of wet noodles as they both tried to get their breathing under control. Jules recovered first and reached down to tilt Bobby's face up to his. Thank you didn't seem to be the right thing to say, but neither did words of love. Jules bit his lip and grinned. "You're pretty damn good at that."

Bobby chuckled. "You ain't seen nothing yet."

Chapter Six

By the time Jules arrived, the boat reconstruction project appeared to be in full swing. He climbed out of his Jaguar and walked towards Bobby, who was busy fixing a board to the hull of the boat.

He waved to the other men, as he approached his lover. "Sorry I'm late."

Bobby's head turned his way and Jules was blessed with one of those million dollar smiles. "You're here now, that's the important thing."

Although Bobby's hands were busy, he pursed his lips. "Give me a kiss to last until I can get at you for real."

Jules took a step closer and pressed his body against Bobby's, lightly brushing the front of his lover's faded work jeans. Leaning in, he covered Bobby's lips and slipped his tongue inside, tasting beer.

As their kiss continued, both men seemed to forget about the others. Bobby moaned and attacked Jules' mouth like he was starving for it.

A throat cleared, and Jules opened his eyes. He released Bobby's tongue and grinned. "I'm suddenly dying for a beer."

"In the cooler up on deck," Bobby whispered against Jules' lips. "Give me twenty minutes, and I'll come greet you properly."

"Any more proper and the two of you might as well head to bed," Marco laughed.

Jules looked Bobby up and down. The tight jeans and white muscle shirt made him horny as hell. Funny, he'd never really been into the blue-collar-type of guy, but Bobby was positively drool-worthy.

Licking his lips, Jules gazed into Bobby's eyes. "What would you like me to do?"

Leaning in, Bobby whispered in Jules' ear. "I'd really like you to get on your knees and suck my cock, but I don't think these guys would appreciate it much."

Jules scanned the group of handsome men. "Probably not. Pity, because the idea sounds absolutely delicious."

Bobby's eyebrows rose. "This is a side of you I'm quickly coming to enjoy."

"Really? What side?"

"The sex machine side. I thought you'd be a kind and loving partner, but I had no idea you'd be such a hell-cat."

Jules laughed. He'd never been called a hell-cat in his entire life. He may have enjoyed sex in the past, but he'd never felt like fucking at all hours of the day, at least not until he started spending time with Bobby.

He wondered if it had to do with him getting older? Was he trying to recapture his youth? No, that couldn't be it. Although he and Morgan had enjoyed an active sex life, it had never been Jules' priority.

"Come find me as soon as you can," Jules said with a wink and climbed the ladder to board the boat.

He could hear Bobby's friends' teasing comments as he went down the stairs to the salon. There, he found Eric and Angelo applying varnish to the already sanded bulkhead. "Looks good."

Eric turned and smiled. "It does, doesn't it? I think Bobby'll be happy when he sees it."

Jules bent over and retrieved a bottle of beer from the cooler. "Where do you need me?"

Eric stopped and glanced around the cabin. "Well, you could start carrying the furniture on deck if you want to. I think Kent talked Bobby into replacing the deck flooring instead of trying to fix it."

Jules took another pull off his beer and set the bottle on one of the built-in shelves. He worked for the next thirty minutes carrying everything he could. The narrow sofa he'd need help with, although looking at it, Jules thought it might be better to junk it. The chairs were in good structural condition, some new upholstery and they'd be good as new, but the sofa was another story.

He thought about the buttery yellow leather couch he had in the den. He never even bothered going into the room. Jules wondered if Bobby would be offended if he offered to give it to him. His lover would have to come up with a way to attach the legs to the floor, but Jules doubted it would be a problem.

A sweaty set of arms wrapped around Jules from behind. "Hey, baby."

Turning his head, Jules kissed his man. "Break time?"

"Mmm hmm," Bobby moaned, rimming Jules' lips with his tongue.

Without another word, Jules took Bobby's hand and led him back to the captain's cabin. Once he had the door shut, he pushed Bobby onto the bed and straddled his lap. Grinding his erection against Bobby's, Jules groaned. "I've been thinking about this for two full days."

He dug into his pocket and handed Bobby a single-use packet of lube and a condom. Jules pulled his tight T-shirt up until it sat just below his armpits and went to work on his jeans.

Standing, he stepped out of his shoes and shucked his jeans and underwear. When he noticed that Bobby hadn't moved, he ran a hand up his torso to rub across his pebbled nipples. "Not interested?"

"Course I'm interested, just enjoying the show." Bobby reached down and unzipped his jeans. "Help me with my boots, will ya?"

With his erection bobbing up and down as he moved, Jules untied Bobby's work boots and pulled them off. "So what'd you do last night?"

Bobby kicked off his jeans and scooted back on the bed. "Well, since my personal sex machine wasn't available, I was left working on the boat."

Jules picked the packet of lube up from the bed and tore it open with his teeth. After squirting the contents into his hand, he straddled Bobby's lap and started stretching himself. Never in his adult life had he

208

wanted someone to fuck him as bad as he did at that moment. His fingers were shaking with impatience as he started with two, and quickly worked up to four.

By the time Bobby's erection was sheathed, Jules was out of patience. He reached behind him and held Bobby's cock by the base as he impaled himself. "Oh, god, yes," he moaned, dropping his head back.

The delicious feel of Bobby's fat length filling him had Jules ready to come in no time. He held on, by sheer will as he rode his lover's shaft.

Although Bobby seemed quiet, his expression signalled his obvious enjoyment. Dropping to Bobby's chest, Jules kissed him. "You have no idea how much I needed this."

Bobby chuckled, thrusting up. "I think I've got a pretty good idea."

Jules continued to ride the thick cock, knowing Bobby really did have no idea. Since the bottom-boy in him had been reawakened, he'd thought of nothing else but Bobby's dick inside of him. He could be right in the middle of something at work, and his asshole would twitch with the need to be filled. He'd often wondered whether he was going through some kind of midlife crisis.

Reaching between their bodies, Jules wrapped a hand around his cock. He wished he could tell Bobby how much he thought of him during any given day. Sometimes he worried that he'd become obsessed by the man, but then he'd push the negative thoughts away. There was nothing unhealthy about the way he felt about Bobby. Even if he couldn't confess those feelings, they were indeed valid.

Pushing Jules to the side, Bobby rolled over on top of him. "My turn."

Spreading his legs as wide as a forty-three year old man could, Jules happily gave his body over to Bobby's thrusting hips.

"Yes, oh, shit, yes," he continued to mumble.

The first rope of his seed landed high on his chest as his cock erupted. The way Bobby rode his ass, Jules had no doubt he'd feel like the man was still inside of him for days to come.

Bobby's orgasm seemed to take him by surprise. His eyes opened wide and his jaw dropped in a silent scream. He continued to thrust his way through his climax, grinding his pelvis against Jules' ass.

Collapsing on top of Jules, Bobby panted, his breath heating the skin of Jules' neck. "You're gonna kill me," Bobby croaked.

Bobby's body tensed and he rose up on his elbows to peer down at Jules. "I'm sorry. That was a shitty thing to say."

Jules hadn't even realised what Bobby had said until the apology. He shook his head. "It took me a long time to understand that I wasn't responsible for Morgan's death. Don't apologise."

* * * *

Bobby rolled to the side and rested his hands on his chest. Why would Jules ever feel responsible for Morgan's death? He realised he didn't know the whole story, something he'd definitely have to remedy in the coming months.

Turning to gaze into Jules' eyes, he smiled. "I haven't had this much sex since I was in high school."

Jules' brows rose to his hairline. "You had sex in high school?"

"Sure, I went to an all male boarding school. That's what you do to pass the time."

Jules whistled. "I didn't have my first sexual experience until I went away to college."

As much as it twisted his gut to think about Jules with another man, he knew this was his chance to delve deeper into the relationship with Morgan. "Morgan?"

Bobby couldn't read the expression on Jules' face. "Uh, yeah. We met during our freshman year."

So, Morgan was Jules' first lover. Bobby wondered if that had anything to do with the hold the dead man still had over Jules. "Have you dated much since..."

"No, not really. I tried going out, meeting guys at bars and stuff. Even hired an escort once, but they always left me feeling...empty."

"And now?" Bobby pushed.

Jules rolled over on his side and stroked Bobby's sweaty chest. "Now, I've found you."

Bobby covered Jules' hand, stilling it against his chest. "I'm not the rebound guy, am I?"

"Rebound guy? Morgan's been dead for sixteen years."

Bobby shook his head. "Doesn't matter how long he's been gone. I'm just worried that this is the first time you've opened yourself to a relationship since his death."

What he didn't say was that he'd been worried things were progressing too fast between them. The more he felt himself fall for Jules, the more scared he became. He knew from talking to Zac and Eric just how new dating was for Jules. Bobby wasn't sure his heart could stand to be broken by the man, and with Jules' apparent zeal for constant sex, it was even more worrisome.

What if he was being used? A rich man's play toy? He didn't think Jules would hurt him on purpose. He felt he knew enough about the guy to determine that, but what if Jules wasn't even aware of Bobby's growing feelings?

His thoughts were interrupted by his chirping cell phone. "Sorry, hang on." Sitting up, he reached for his jeans with one hand as he slid the condom off with the other.

Glancing at the display, he groaned. "What do you want?"

"You to pull your head out of your ass and get back on *The Gypsy*," Brad barked.

"I quit, or couldn't you tell by the lack of my things on the boat?"

"You can't quit. This is a family operation and you're family."

Bobby wrapped the condom in a tissue and tossed it into the trash can. He ran a hand over Jules' hip to calm himself. "You lied to me, Brad. Why the hell would I want to work for two deceitful sons-of-bitches? You and Dad wanted *The Gypsy* bad enough to take her from me, well, she's your problem now. Don't call me again."

Bobby turned off his phone and tossed it back onto his jeans.

"Problem?" Jules asked, pulling Bobby down into his arms.

"Nothing I didn't anticipate." He gave Jules a deep kiss, running his hands over the man's naked, sticky body.

"I need to get back out there before I lose my workforce." He sat up again and swung his legs over the side of the bed and reached for his clothes.

"Want me to run out and get something for everyone to eat?" Jules asked.

"You don't have to do that. We can order pizza or something."

"I don't mind, really. I know a great barbeque place. I'll just pick up some meat and bread, couple of side dishes."

Bobby pulled his boots on and tied them. "I'd appreciate it."

"Oh, really? How much?" Jules said, bending one leg up in a seductive pose.

Bobby bent over and sucked Jules' flaccid cock into his mouth. The longer he sucked, the harder the shaft became. Knowing he didn't have time to finish what he'd started, he released the cock and smiled.

"I'll think of something."

* * * *

As soon as he kissed Jules goodbye the harassment began.

"You're becoming quite the lover boy," Marco chuckled.

"Shut up," Bobby barked.

"What? You suck his tongue in front of us and we can't comment?" Kent teased.

Bobby put his hands on his hips. He wasn't upset with his friends for giving him a hard time. He deserved it after the display he and Jules had put on earlier, but if he didn't at least offer a token protest, they'd know he was falling in love.

Love? Bobby shook the thought away and grabbed a beer out of the cooler. "Give me a break, will ya? It's been ages since I've dated anyone I'd be willing to bring around you Neanderthals."

His friends chuckled again but eventually went back to work on the hull of the boat. Eric walked over and leaned his back against the boat with a broad grin on his face.

"You really like him, don't you?"

Bobby took a drink of his beer and nodded. "We've got a few issues to work out, but yeah."

"I don't know him real well, but I can honestly say I've never seen Dr. Peters happier. I'm not the only one who's noticed either. He's kinda the talk of the ER department lately, especially after you rode in on your white horse after he passed out and bumped his head."

That brought up a subject Bobby had been meaning to ask Eric about. "What made Jules faint that day?"

Eric broke eye contact. "Have you asked him?"

"Yeah, but he never really gave me an answer."

When Eric continued to just stand there, Bobby put a hand on the smaller man's shoulder. "Tell me."

Eric shook his head. "I don't know anything for sure."

"Then tell me what you think?" Bobby prodded.

Eric bit his lower lip as he suddenly seemed to find his shoes fascinating. "I think maybe the guy I was working on reminded him of Morgan. I don't know that for sure though, so don't say anything. All I know is Dr. Peters took one look at the patient and went white, seconds before passing out."

"Maybe he knew the guy," Bobby offered.

Eric shook his head. "He didn't. The patient was from Little Rock, here on business. It was a rental car that he wrecked."

Bobby set down his beer and picked up the electric sander and a mask. "Thanks for telling me."

Eric started to walk off but stopped and turned around. "If it helps, I think he really likes you."

Bobby nodded. "It does."

He watched as Eric retreated back up the ladder, before turning his attention to the hull. Eric's theory made sense, especially after the scene in the bedroom with Morgan's photographs. Had Bobby known Morgan was forefront in Jules' mind that day he never would've initiated sex between them. He may be the jealous type, but he sure as hell wasn't a cold-hearted bastard.

"Sorry, but I need to take off," Trey said, tapping Bobby on the shoulder.

He turned off the sander and lowered his mask. "Why, hot date?"

Trey snorted. "Hardly. I promised I'd chaperone prom."

There was no greater torture in Bobby's opinion. He'd never understand why Zac and Trey chose to spend their days with high school kids. He couldn't stand the smart-assed fuckers. "Have fun with that."

Trey grinned and strode towards his car.

"Where's he going?" Zac asked.

"Said he was chaperoning prom." Bobby gave an exaggerated shudder.

Zac smiled. "So he did sign up after all. Good for him."

"Yeah, if it's such a great gig, why aren't you there?" Bobby questioned.

"Because I don't have a crush on the principal."

That was news to Bobby. Hell, he didn't think he'd ever even known to look twice at a man, let alone have a crush. He knew Trey was gay, you could tell that just by being in his company for more than five minutes, but as far as he knew, his friend never dated.

"Interesting."

* * * *

Jules watched Bobby as he put away the last of the tools. Working in the sun all day had turned his skin a subtle shade of brown. Jules licked his lips as Bobby bent over his toolbox. He couldn't resist any longer. He'd been good for the rest of the evening, trying his best to keep his hands off the gorgeous man in front of him, but now it was just the two of them.

Jules stood and walked over to Bobby. Running both hands over his lover's ass, he groaned. "Are we through for the day?"

Bobby stood and turned around to take Jules into his embrace. "We're done working if that's what you mean."

Jules ran his hands up Bobby's muscled arms to clasp behind his neck. "I'm off tomorrow, but I'm still on call so I need to be close to the hospital. You feel like going home with me? We can wake up and read the Sunday paper in bed."

Bobby ground his groin against Jules. "I can think of a few other things I'd rather do in bed than read."

"Really? You'll have to show me," Jules teased, kissing the base of Bobby's throat.

Bobby moaned and took a step back. "Mind if I grab a change of clothes?"

"Not at all."

Jules waited while Bobby gathered his things. He heard a car pull up outside and went up to investigate. A well-dressed business man got out of an expensive car and sneered at *My Second Chance*. The sinking feeling in Jules' stomach told him exactly who the man was. Without saying a word, Jules went below deck and to the captain's cabin.

"I think maybe your brother's here."

Bobby stopped in the midst of shoving a clean pair of jeans into a small duffle. "Brad?"

Jules shrugged. "I don't know for sure. Does he drive a grey Mercedes sedan?"

"Shit." Bobby tossed the bag on the bed and headed for the deck.

Jules wasn't sure if he should follow Bobby or stay put. He decided to stay far enough out of sight that Brad wouldn't make any derogatory comments. He wasn't sure how Bobby's family felt about his sexual preference or if they even knew. It definitely seemed to Jules that the family wasn't close.

Jules sat on the deck out of site from the two men arguing below.

"What do you want, Brad?"

"I told you earlier on the phone. I need you to pull your head out of your ass and get back to work."

"I don't work for you and Dad anymore, or didn't you get the resignation letter I left on *The Gypsy*?"

"Don't be an ass. You and I both know you can't just walk away from *The Gypsy*. Come on back, and we'll forget this misunderstanding happened."

"Fuck you. You've never treated me with anything more than contempt. I wouldn't work for you and Dad if you paid me double. You're both lying sacks of shit as far as I'm concerned."

Jules felt like an intruder. He got to his feet and started to head back below deck. The problems between Bobby and his family evidently went beyond Brad buying *The Gypsy*. He caught snatches of conversation as he descended the steps.

"We can't find anyone else to captain her," Brad whined.

"That's your problem."

"Do you want us to sell her? Is that it?" Brad asked.

Jules paused on the stairs only to hear Bobby let loose with a string of very colourful curse words.

He heard a car door slam and quickly sat on a five-gallon paint bucket. Bobby's face was beet red. Jules started to say something, but Bobby held up a hand, stopping him.

"Give me a few minutes, will ya?" Bobby asked and disappeared into his cabin.

Jules wasn't sure how long he sat there, before the door finally opened and Bobby came striding out, duffle in hand.

"You ready?" he asked.

Jules nodded and led the way to his car. "You want to ride with me, or follow?" he asked.

Bobby tossed his bag into his Jeep and continued walking until he was nose to nose with Jules. "I'll follow, but first things first."

He wrapped his arms around Jules and kissed him. Jules opened immediately for his lover's questing tongue. The fervour with which Bobby kissed him, told Jules the man was looking for a little reassurance.

"Are you sure you don't want to ride with me? I promise not to hold you hostage, chained to my bed."

Bobby grinned. "Yeah, I'll ride with ya."

Bobby walked over to his Jeep and picked up his bag. After tossing it in the backseat of Jules' car, he leaned over for another kiss. "We can discuss the chains later."

Chapter Seven

After slipping on his boxer-briefs, Bobby started downstairs. His ringing cell phone had him turning back to the bedroom. "Hello?"

"Bobby, it's Mom."

Bobby hadn't spoken to his mother since the day of the blow-up. "Hi, Mom."

"I was wondering if you were free for lunch this afternoon?"

Running a hand through his hair, he thought of the sexy man making breakfast for him. "Sorry, I've already got plans. Maybe sometime this week."

His mom sighed. "What's so important that you can't have a short lunch with your mother?"

Had his mother ever bothered putting him first in her life, the comment might have made Bobby feel bad, but that wasn't the case. "I'm spending the day with a friend."

"A boyfriend?" she inquired.

"Yes, if you must know."

"Oh, don't act like that, young man. You know I've never cared about your sexual orientation."

That's because you never really cared, period. "Whatever."

"Maybe your boyfriend would like to have lunch with us. I'd be willing to allow him to join us."

Sitting on the side of the bed, Bobby fell back. His mom really sounded like she was trying to bridge the gap between them. She'd never offered to meet any of the men he'd dated. "I'll have to talk to Jules and call you back."

"That's fine, dear. Just let me know as soon as you can."

Bobby hung up and noticed he had two messages. When he saw they were from Brad, he deleted them without listening. The last thing he needed was to be cussed out by his prick brother again.

Tossing the phone on the bed, he went downstairs. "Something smells good."

"There you are. I was getting ready to send a search party." Jules, dressed in a thin cotton knee-length robe, took two plates out of the warming drawer and set them on the table.

After taking several bites, Bobby glanced up at Jules. "My mom called. She wants the two of us to meet her for lunch."

He took a sip of coffee as Jules seemed to think it over. "Did she actually say she wanted to meet me?"

Bobby shrugged and swallowed a piece of bacon. "She asked if I'd invite you to join us. I guess that means she wants to meet you."

"What do you suppose she'll think about the age difference?" Jules asked.

"All I have to do is introduce you as Dr. Peters, and she'll be fine with it. My mother has always been about appearances and social status. Funny since she was my father's secretary when he fucked her and got her pregnant with me."

Jules wiped his mouth with a napkin. "Was your father married at the time?"

Bobby nodded. "Yep, to Brad's mother. I guess it was kind of a big deal at the time. Brad's mother came from money. The same money my father used to start his company. I think it's one of the reasons Brad hates me so much."

Jules got up and stood beside Bobby. Knowing what his lover wanted, Bobby scooted his chair back and Jules straddled his lap. Burying his fingers in Bobby's hair, Jules kissed him.

"I'd love to meet your mother, but only if you want me to."

Bobby untied the knot at Jules' waist and parted the robe for his questing hands. "I'm not exactly sure what she might be up to, but I would like her to meet you."

Bobby skimmed his hands down Jules' back to cup the globes of his bare ass. Bringing one of his hands back up to the table, he ran his fingers through the butter dish.

"What're you doing?" Jules asked.

Chuckling, Bobby entered Jules' puckered hole with one buttered digit. "Trying to butter you up."

Jules rolled his eyes and nipped Bobby's lower lip. "That was bad."

Introducing another finger, Bobby bit Jules' back. "Oh, I can be even badder."

"So can I," Jules replied, pulling a condom out of the pocket of his robe.

* * * *

Getting into the passenger seat of the 1956 Jaguar, Bobby pointed to the last garage bay where another car sat covered. "What's that?"

Jules didn't even look as he started the car. "That was my first restoration project."

"Cool. Can I see it?"

Bobby noticed the way Jules' fingers gripped the steering wheel as he pulled out of the garage.

"Perhaps someday," Jules said and left it at that.

It was a beautiful day. The sun was actually shining, something rare for that time of year. They'd decided to swing by Bobby's on the way home from lunch. He wanted to see if the hull was ready for a new coat of paint.

"Are we going to be late?" Jules asked.

"No. Mom's always at least twenty minutes fashionably late for everything anyway."

They parked in front of the upscale café and were seated on the patio. Bobby wanted to order a drink, but decided it would be best to keep his wits. He never knew what frame of mind his mother might be in and he wanted his full faculties to deal with any situation.

Jules reached over and threaded his fingers through Bobby's. "I can't believe I'm nervous."

Bobby chuckled. "I'll protect you."

Leaning over, Bobby gave Jules a chaste kiss on the lips. He spotted his mother's two-toned grey Rolls Royce as it pulled up to the curb. Her driver jumped out and opened the car door. "She's here."

Jules looked over and whistled. "Arriving in style."

"It's the only way she travels."

His mother swept onto the patio in her designer clothes and offered her cheek. Bobby gave his mom the customary greeting and gestured towards Jules. "Katherine Quinn, I'd like to introduce you to Dr. Jules Peters."

Like he knew she would, Bobby's mother's eyes sparkled as she held out her hand. Jules was as smooth as ever and bent to place a kiss on the back of Katherine's hand.

"A pleasure to meet you, Katherine."

Bobby stood and pulled out his mother's chair. Once they were seated, he called the waiter over. "Would you care for something to drink?" he asked his mom.

"Sparkling water with a lime twist."

Bobby rolled his eyes. "Just bring me plain water, no twist."

"I'll have the same," Jules agreed.

Bobby noticed his mother staring at Jules. "So how've you been, mom?"

"Dreadful," she answered.

The waiter came back with our drinks and asked if we were ready to order.

"Give us a few more minutes," his mom instructed.

After the waiter left, she turned to Bobby. "You simply must end this tiff you're having with Bradley and your father."

Bobby choked on sip of water and began coughing. Jules reached over and put his hand on Bobby's thigh. Recovering, he stared at his mother. "Is that why you wanted to meet me for lunch?"

Katherine made a tsking sound. "I care about my family. You being at odds with your brother and father is having serious repercussions on my marriage, and I won't have it."

Bobby couldn't believe what he was hearing. "So you're blaming me?"

"I'm not blaming anyone. Bradley said that he attempted to clear the air with you, but you refused to listen."

Putting his arms on the table, Bobby leaned forward. "Stay out of this, Mom."

Katherine squared her shoulders. "I can't stay out of it. Quinn Industries isn't doing well. The board of directors fired Bradley last month and according to your father, the board is trying to see him fired as well. Your father has had to hire a very expensive attorney in order to try and hold his place as head of the corporation."

Bobby was shocked that Brad had been booted out of the company. He'd always been Quinn Industries' golden boy. "What does any of this have to do with me?"

"As you can imagine, the upkeep and marina fees for *The Gypsy* are quite expensive. Without that damn boat bringing in money, soon your father and brother will be forced to sell it. Is that what you want?"

Yes, that's exactly what I want. "Tell you what, mother. Go back to dear old Dad and tell him I'll take

The Gypsy off his hands for twenty-five thousand dollars and not a penny more."

"Don't be ridiculous. *The Gypsy* is worth at least five times that amount of money."

"Now, yes. After I broke my back restoring her. But Brad and Dad bought it from the bank for what I still owed on the loan which was twenty thousand, four hundred and eighty-seven dollars. Hell, I'm giving them thirteen dollars profit."

Bobby noticed Jules' hand pressed against his mouth in an attempt not to laugh. He winked at his lover. At this point, he didn't care if he got *The Gypsy* back or not. He'd probably just turn around and sell her again anyway.

His mother stood and picked her clutch bag up from the table. "You're being an ass, Robert."

"Maybe so, but it's what they deserve. Let 'em try and sell it. It'll take months and in the meantime, they'll keep racking up marina fees and repair costs."

Bobby crossed his arms, and watched his mother walk away. He turned to Jules and shrugged. "Lovely, isn't she?"

"How did you turn out so normal?" Jules asked with a chuckle.

"I was fortunate enough to be sent away to boarding school when I was eight."

Bobby took another drink of his water. In the beginning, he'd hated boarding school. All he wanted was to go home, but his parents wouldn't allow it. They'd told him it was for the best. Unlike most kids at the school, his parents only allowed him one visit a year at Christmas break. During the summers he'd been sent to camp. By the time he was a teenager,

Bobby couldn't have cared less about his family and they'd seemed to reciprocate those feelings.

The more he thought about his mother's plea, the angrier he became. "Mind if we get out of here? We can grab something to eat on the way."

Jules stood and tossed some money on the table. "Let's go."

As soon as they were away from the restaurant, Jules pulled into a small Italian place. "I'll run in and get us something to go."

Bobby nodded. Before getting out of the car, Jules pulled him in for a kiss. Bobby returned the gesture with interest, delving his tongue deep into Jules' mouth. "Thanks."

Jules ran his knuckles down the side of Bobby's face. It was probably the tenderest gesture anyone had ever given him. Bobby turned his head and kissed his lover's fingers.

Without saying anything, Jules got out of the car and went inside. As Bobby sat there, he started thinking about both *The Gypsy* and *My Second Chance*. He had indeed loved his first boat. When he'd lost the trawler to Brad, it had almost killed him. He purchased *My Second Chance* as a way of getting over the pain. But what he was quickly coming to realise was that nothing would heal the hurt dealt him by losing his first love to Brad and his father.

Jules came back and handed a bag full of containers to Bobby before getting in. Peeking into the bag, Bobby grinned. "Hungry?"

Jules shrugged and started the car. "This way we don't have to go out again later."

They drove to the construction yard, and pulled up beside *My Second Chance*. Bobby tried to imagine what the boat would look like when finished. He got out of the low-slung car and ran his hand over the hull.

"Is it ready?" Jules asked from behind him.

"Yeah, but I don't feel like doing it right now." Bobby wasn't positive that he'd ever feel like it.

"Ready to eat?"

Bobby turned back to Jules. "Yeah."

Once in the salon, he made a makeshift table and chairs out of paint buckets and a sheet of wood.

"The woodwork in here turned out nice," Jules commented.

Bobby studied the shiny walls. Before he'd started, years of grime had masked the wood's true beauty, now the mahogany panels were indeed breathtaking. "She's cleaning up pretty nice."

"I'll say."

Once he got the floor laid, it was just a matter of getting the furniture reupholstered. The engine had been one of the first things he'd tackled, so other than a tune-up, it should be good to go.

Bobby ate a bite of spaghetti. Why wasn't he more excited at the prospect of finishing *My Second Chance*? The scene with his mother continued to bother him. Maybe that was the reason his desire to finish the boat had waned.

"Have your parents always been that way?" Jules asked, breaking into Bobby's thoughts.

"What way? Putting money first? Yeah."

Jules' hand landed on his shoulder. "Not all wealthy people are like that, you know. My sister and I had plenty of love growing up."

"You were lucky," Bobby mumbled.

"I know, but I don't think I realised it as much as I do now."

"What were they like?"

Jules swallowed a piece of bread and took a drink of water before answering. "I don't know. Don't get me wrong. I mean, my dad didn't coach my baseball team or anything like that, but they were always at the games. I think maybe my dad grew up in a house like the one you did, because he seemed to make an extra effort to spend time with me and Beth."

Bobby wondered if he'd be a different person had his parents spent time with him. He shook his head. No sense dwelling on a past that couldn't be relived.

"Mind if we go back to your place? My heart's just not in this at the moment."

"I've got a better idea. Why don't we do something fun, like go to the zoo?" Jules asked.

"The zoo?"

"Yeah, come on. It should be open for at least another three hours. That should give us plenty of time to meet your relatives in the monkey cage."

"Har, har." Bobby scratched his head. He didn't want to admit it to Jules, but he'd never been to the zoo. He'd never really seen the appeal of looking at a bunch of animals that you could see on television. Still, he knew Jules was doing his best to cheer him up. "Okay."

"Good, finish your lunch and let's go."

* * * *

Jules handed Bobby his hotdog. "Do you want to sit?"

Bobby shook his head. "We've only got another thirty minutes before the park closes. Let's see if we can find the reptile house."

Jules hid his grin and walked along side of Bobby. His lover had reminded him of a kid since they'd been there. At first Bobby had tried to put on a cool act, but that fell by the wayside as soon as he spotted the seals.

They must've watched those damn little guys for at least thirty minutes before he was finally able to drag Bobby away. To see a grown man take such joy in something as simple as watching an elephant eat a cube of frozen fruit, threw him. Jules began to wonder just how alienated from a normal childhood Bobby had been.

"Wouldn't you rather see the polar bears?" he asked.

Bobby's eyes lit up. "They have polar bears? Isn't it too hot for them?"

Jules grinned. "They have a special habitat for them."

"Cool. Is it on the way to the reptile house?"

Jules stopped and tossed his napkin in a trash can. "What's with you and snakes?"

Bobby shrugged. "I like 'em. When I was a boy I was obsessed with them. I read everything I could get my hands on."

Finally. A sign that Bobby had actually been a boy. "Did you have one?"

"A snake? No way. Headmaster Jorgens would never have allowed it. I did find one at camp though. I kept it in a box under my bed until it escaped." Bobby threw his trash away and took Jules' hand.

Jules threaded their fingers together and squeezed. "If you think this zoo is good, we should take a trip to San Diego some weekend. Have you ever been to Sea World?"

"No. Why? You wanna go with me?"

"Yeah. They've got an awesome sea lion show that I think you'd love. We could do the zoo thing and Sea World in the same weekend."

"Sounds like a plan."

* * * *

"Hey."

Bobby tossed an armload of scrap lumber into the dumpster and turned to find Marco headed his way. "You working this site?"

"Yeah, just got here. Doing some brick work out on the patio." Marco gave Bobby a friendly hug. "How've you been?"

Bobby shrugged. "Work sucks, but everything else is okay. You?"

"Same shit different day," Marco replied.

"You boys gonna talk or are you planning to actually get some work done?" Kent asked, strolling past.

Marco rolled his eyes. "Better get to it. Meet me for lunch?"

"Sure, although I'm brown bagging it."

"Same here. I'll meet you under that shade tree over there around eleven-thirty."

Bobby nodded his agreement and grabbed the wheelbarrow handles. As he went to retrieve another load of scrap, he began wondering what the hell he was doing there. He'd been educated in some of the finest schools in the country and he was working as a labourer on a construction site.

Maybe I should go back and finish college?

"Bobby," someone yelled.

Bobby glanced over his shoulder. "Yeah?" he asked one of the electricians.

"We're all done on the first floor."

"Okay, I'll be in as soon as I finish with this pile."

He began loading more scrap into the wheelbarrow. College was looking better all the time.

* * * *

It was Thursday evening before Bobby saw Jules again. He had a new appreciation for Zac's patience with Eric's work schedule. He pulled into the garage using the remote door opener that Jules had given him the previous Sunday and shut off the engine.

The door leading to the house opened and Jules appeared with two bottles of his favourite beer. "Thirsty?"

Bobby smiled for the first time all week. "Yeah."

His relationship with Jules was the one thing that kept him going. He got out of the Jeep, duffle in hand and walked towards his lover. Standing toe to toe with Jules, Bobby leaned in for a kiss. "I've missed you."

Jules returned his smile and motioned towards the kitchen. "I stopped on the way home and picked up some dinner. You hungry?"

"Starved." Bobby followed Jules into the house and set his bag at the base of the staircase.

"I hope Chinese is okay." Jules began opening cartons as Bobby joined him at the table.

"Sure."

On the drive from the construction site, Bobby tried to figure out what to do next. Should he complete *My Second Chance* and sell her, or pull his head out of his ass and captain her?

Bobby wanted to confide in his lover. Maybe if they talked about what was bothering him, Jules could give him a different point of view.

"I don't think I wanna finish the boat," he confessed.

With a forkful of beef and broccoli halfway to his mouth, Jules paused. "Why?"

Bobby shrugged and pushed his plate away. "I guess my heart's just not in it."

Jules set his fork down. "What will you do? Continue to work for Kent?"

The idea of spending the rest of his life doing construction held no appeal. "I don't know. Maybe I should go back to school."

"Okay. Anything in particular you're interested in?" Jules asked, finally taking his bite of food.

Boats. Bobby sighed and ran his fingers through his hair. "I don't know. To be honest, I can't imagine doing anything else. Guess I'll need to think about it."

"What about the offer for *The Gypsy* you told your mother about?"

"I doubt they'll take it. Hell, even if they did, I'd probably turn around and put her up for sale."

Bobby watched as Jules continued to eat his dinner. After swallowing the last bite of food, he set his plate aside and regarded Bobby. "What was the favourite part of your job?"

"Huh?"

"When were you the happiest?" Jules prodded.

"Oh, that's easy. Taking families and groups like that out, but you don't make the same kind of money."

Scooting his chair over, Jules pushed Bobby's plate in front of him. "Eat while you listen."

Surprised at the command, Bobby stuck a bite of cashew chicken into his mouth.

"Now," Jules began, "how much money do you need to pay your bills and make you happy?"

Bobby took another bite of food as he thought about the question. He didn't have a figure of course, but he understood where Jules was going. Would it even be possible to book enough charters to hold the cost down? Because he knew that's what it would take. The kind of groups he enjoyed being around couldn't afford the high prices he'd been charging while working for Brad, but if he moved the boat to one of the more out of the way marinas it might be possible.

He leaned against Jules and grinned. "I've been worrying about this all week. How is it that you can put everything into perspective in a matter of fifteen minutes?"

"It's a gift," Jules chuckled.

Cupping Bobby's chin, Jules turned it towards him. "I've fallen in love with a great guy who doesn't seem to know his own worth. You've seen firsthand that money can't buy happiness. Hell, I'm proof of that. Doing what you love is what feeds the soul."

Bobby leaned in for a kiss, slipping his tongue into Jules mouth. "You love me?"

It was the first time Jules had said those words. Bobby had definitely fallen in love with the man in his arms, but he'd been too chicken shit to say anything.

"What's not to love?"

Without a word, Bobby stood and pulled Jules to his feet. He led him up the stairs and to the bedroom. He wanted so much to say the words back to Jules, but he wanted it to be special. It was the first time in his life that he'd professed love and he hoped like hell he could do it.

Once they were both undressed and under the covers, Bobby slid on top of his man and looked him in the eyes. "You're everything I've ever wanted in a partner. I have my bad days and the way my life is going, I'll never be rich, but..."

Jules grabbed the back of Bobby's head and pulled him down for a kiss. As their tongues played, their cocks rubbed against each other. Breaking the kiss, Bobby looked down into the eyes of the man who meant everything to him. "I love you."

There, he'd said it and surprisingly, it wasn't hard at all. Funny how those three words could make a man feel so incredibly bound to another human being.

Jules inhaled and a wide grin spread across his face as he thrust up against Bobby. With a wicked grin, Bobby slid down his lover's body and took Jules' erection into his mouth. He loved the smell and taste of Jules' cock.

Before starting on the head, Bobby worked his tongue up and down the length a few times before nuzzling Jules' balls with his nose and mouth. He lapped at the area long enough that Jules began to squirm.

"Suck me," Jules begged, gripping a handful of Bobby's hair.

With a groan, Bobby licked his way up Jules' shaft to the dripping mushroom head. Taking the first couple of inches into his mouth, Bobby gave the crown a tongue bath, making sure to press against the sensitive underside.

He was rewarded with a constant flow of pre-cum as he began to take more of the fat cock into his mouth. When the head touched the back of his throat he stopped. Deep-throating a cock was a turn-on for some men, but he preferred to pleasure the first few inches. After all, the aim of a blow-job was giving pleasure to your partner, not seeing how much sausage you could stuff down your throat. He seemed to be doing a fair job at making Jules feel good, because his man was going crazy under him.

The grip on Bobby's hair became almost painful and he knew Jules was close. He scraped the sensitive underside with his bottom teeth and opened wide. Right on cue, Bobby was rewarded with long bursts of the thick cream he loved so much as Jules yelled his name to the ceiling.

Bobby didn't think he'd ever tire of hearing his partner call his name in climax. After licking Jules clean, Bobby crawled up the bed and dug in the drawer for the lube. "My turn."

Chapter Eight

Friday evening, Bobby pulled into the garage, disappointed to see Jules wasn't home yet. Going into the man's house without him there just didn't seem right somehow, so he figured he'd just hang out until his lover arrived.

Getting out of the Jeep, he wandered over to the far bay. He'd been curious about the car under the cover for a while, but had yet to investigate. Bobby lifted the tarpaulin and whistled. The gold 1978 Firebird Trans Am surprised him. It seemed totally out of character for Jules.

He pushed the cover back further and opened the door. Folding himself into the driver's seat, Bobby looked around. Even the interior was in mint condition, though he expected nothing less.

He noticed a fine layer of dust on the dash, and decided to do something about it. Going over to the cabinets beside Jules' work bench, Bobby found a rag and some stuff to make the interior shine.

About halfway through the project, the garage door opened and Jules pulled in.

"Hey, babe," Bobby greeted, climbing out of the Firebird.

"What the fuck do you think you're doing?" Jules screamed, getting out of his Jaguar.

Shocked by the vehemence in Jules' tone, Bobby held up the rag. "I got here early, so I thought I'd help you out and dust."

Jules rushed towards Bobby and pushed him away from the car. "You have no right to touch something that doesn't belong to you!"

Feeling as if he'd been punched in the face, Bobby dropped the rag and the bottle of cleaner. He turned on his heels and climbed into his Jeep. Opening the garage door, he stared at Jules who was busy covering the Firebird once again.

"You're no different than the rest of them," he spat.

He peeled out of Jules' fancy-assed driveway and headed home. Why the hell had he believed Jules was different? As long as he shoved his dick up the man's ass, everything was fine, but the minute he touched one of his lover's toys, the ceiling came crashing down. Well, fuck him.

The closer he came to his boat, the less he wanted to be anywhere where Jules could find him. Coming to an intersection, he turned right and headed towards the ocean.

The longer he stayed behind the wheel, the more hurt he became. He wasn't sure how long he drove, but the next thing he knew, he was in Santa Cruz.

Somehow his heart must've known what it needed at that moment. He stopped on the way to his favourite beach and picked up a twelve-pack of beer. Maybe an evening spent getting shit-faced would take away the pain?

With his head resting on his duffle, Bobby stared out at Monterey Bay as he opened yet another beer.

"Sir, you can't sleep here," a man said, walking towards him.

Bobby tried to sit up, but weaved a bit. "I don't think I can drive."

The man in the park uniform put his hands on his hips and stared down at him. "Well, either find someone to drive you, or I'll have to call someone to pick you up. We frown on public intoxication."

"I'm nursing a broken heart," he tried to excuse himself.

"Well nurse it somewhere else."

Bobby could tell by the look in the guy's eyes he wasn't going to cut him any slack. He dug his cell phone out of his pocket and called Zac.

"Hello?" a sleepy voice answered.

"Hi, Eric, is Zac there?"

Bobby heard Eric fumbling with the phone before Zac came on. "Bobby? Something wrong?"

"Yeah. I need a ride," he slurred.

"Where're you at?"

"The beach at Monterey Bay that I like to come to."

He heard Zac curse in the background. "What the hell are you doing all the way down there?"

"Gettin' drunk, but they won't let me sleep here, and I can't drive."

Bobby heard sheets rustle in the background.

"Where's Jules?" Zac asked.

"Who the fuck cares. Will you come get me or not?"

Zac sighed. "Yeah, but you'll owe me big time."

"Can't get blood from a stone, Zac."

"Just go sit in your Jeep. I'll be there as soon as I can."

Bobby hung up and looked at the guy still standing over him. "My friend's driving down to get me."

The man held out his hand and pulled Bobby to his feet. "Make sure you clean up this mess before you leave."

Bobby nodded and the guy walked towards his SUV. Staring down at the beer bottles littering the sand, Bobby shook his head. *How pathetic am I?*

* * * *

"Wake up," Zac grouched, punching Bobby's shoulder.

He opened his eyes and tried to remember where the hell he was. "What?"

"Get your shit and let's go," Zac ordered, going back to his own Jeep.

Bobby stretched and yawned. He grabbed his sandy duffle bag and followed.

"Did you get your keys?" Zac asked.

"Shit." Bobby turned back around and pulled his keys out of the ignition then locked up. Returning to Zac's Jeep, Bobby got in and threw his stuff in the back. "I appreciate this."

Zac put the Jeep into gear and headed back towards Pacifica. "Mind telling me what the hell you're doing in Santa Cruz?"

Bobby rested his head against the back of the seat. "Needed to get away."

"What happened?" Zac asked around a yawn.

"Got my head handed to me for looking at one of Jules' cars."

"Huh? That doesn't sound like him."

"Well, I noticed there was some dust on the dash and stuff so I was cleaning it while waiting for Jules to come home." Bobby shrugged. "Doesn't matter. Better to know what kind of man he is now than later."

"You love him?"

"Yeah."

"Then now is just as bad as later."

* * * *

After spraying a second coat of white paint on the hull, Bobby cleaned out the paint gun and put it away. Sitting around playing poker was the last thing he felt like doing, but he knew his friends would give him hell if he didn't show up.

As he passed by the bed, he reached down and picked up his cell. It didn't surprise him to see that he'd received nine messages in the last four hours. Between his family and Jules, he'd resorted to turning the damn thing off.

He cleared the messages without listening to them and grabbed a change of clothes. Hopefully Marco wouldn't mind sharing Zac's bathroom with him. He needed to get *My Second Chance* finished soon, or he'd be forced to get an apartment.

Bobby left the boat without bothering to take his phone. He'd be around everyone he cared to talk to anyway.

When he arrived at Zac's, he was surprised to see Jules' Jag parked in the driveway. He gripped the Jeep's steering wheel, unsure if he wanted to go in. What the hell was Jules doing here? These were his friends, dammit. Jules had no right. The more he thought about it, the madder he became.

He was just about to go up and give Jules a piece of his mind, when the front door opened and his ex-lover stepped out.

"Go home, Jules," Bobby called up.

"Not until you talk to me," Jules answered, making his way down the steps.

"Nothing to talk about. You put me in my place, and I chose not to put up with it."

As Jules neared, Bobby could see the older man's puffy, red eyes. *Good.* He wasn't the only one who felt like shit.

"I need to apologise and to explain a few things to you."

Bobby shook his head. "Not interested."

He knew Jules would keep on if he stayed where he was, so Bobby snatched the duffle out of the back and shouldered past him.

"Using the shower," he said to Zac as he passed through the living room.

Shutting the bathroom door, Bobby dropped the bag and sat on the side of the tub with his head in his hands. It had almost killed him not to reach out and pull Jules into his arms, but he knew that would be a momentary fix. He simply couldn't live his life with a man who put things above people.

Standing, Bobby undressed and reached in to turn the shower on. He noticed the dirty ring around the tub and couldn't stop a chuckle from erupting. Zac was right. Marco didn't seem to know how to clean up after himself.

As he stepped into the shower, he expected Jules to burst through the door at any moment, but nothing happened. Although he didn't feel like talking to the man, it hurt to know Jules would give up so easily.

After a quick wash-up, Bobby turned off the shower and reached under the sink for the scrub brush. He'd have to remember to give Marco a hard time about his cleaning skills. Once the tub was spotless, he finished dressing and combed his hair.

Opening the door, he was surprised to be met by silence. "Where is everybody?"

He walked through the living room and into the kitchen. Jules sat at the table, hands clenched into a ball. "Where'd everyone go?"

"Outside. They said they weren't letting the two of us out until we talked things out."

"Fuck that," Bobby yelled. He strode to the front door and swung it open. Six men stood on the stairs with their arms crossed. "What the hell's the meaning of this?"

"I'm not going to let you just walk away, Bobby. You owe it to yourself to at least hear what Jules has to say," Zac informed him.

Bobby started to yell at his friends, but snapped his jaws shut. He could tell by the stubborn look on their faces they wouldn't listen anyway. He slammed the door in Zac's face and turned back to the good-looking doctor.

Without saying a word to Jules, he pulled a beer out of the sink.

"The Trans Am was Morgan's," Jules said, his voice so soft Bobby barely heard it.

"What?" Bobby asked, feeling as if a heavy weight had just landed on his chest.

When Jules didn't immediately answer, Bobby went to the table and sat beside him. "Why do you still have Morgan's car?"

Jules began rubbing his watery eyes with the heel of his hand. "He loved that car. Morgan and his dad restored it when he was in school."

Bobby was trying his best to understand why Jules would hold on to the car, but he still didn't get it. "So you couldn't bring yourself to sell it?"

Jules shook his head. "It's worse than that. Morgan was driving that car the night he was killed."

Bobby felt as though all the oxygen had just been sucked from the room. He pictured the other two cars that Jules had painstakingly restored and it suddenly made sense. "You restored it after his funeral, didn't you?"

"Yes."

"Can I ask why?"

Jules shrugged. "Because Morgan was gone, and I had nothing but a twisted hunk of metal to remind me of him. For some reason I thought if I smoothed out the wrinkles and got it running, it would help me get over his death."

"And did it?"

"I guess not since I held onto it for another sixteen years. Until today, that is."

"Today?"

Jules nodded. "I sold it earlier this afternoon."

Bobby swallowed around the lump in his throat. He knew without a doubt that he'd sold the Firebird because of him. What if Jules came to resent him for it?

"Are you sure you were ready to part with it?"

Jules reached out with both hands and threaded his fingers through Bobby's. "I held onto the past for so long, because I had nothing in the present to replace it with. Morgan's gone. I know that. I guess it just made me feel a little less lonely having his things at the house. But I don't need them anymore, because I have something much better than a bunch of pictures and an old car. I have you. Well, hopefully I still have you."

Bobby tugged on Jules' hands, pulling the older man onto his lap. He was still hurt by Jules' actions the previous day, but at least he somewhat understood why he'd reacted the way he did.

"Wanna go home?"

"My place?" Jules asked.

"Yeah." Although that's exactly what he'd meant, Bobby knew he'd probably never come to think of Jules' house as home.

The front door opened and his friends poured into the apartment just as Bobby started kissing his lover. "What the hell? You trap us in here and then don't even give us enough privacy to make up?"

Zac laughed and hit the back of Marco's head. "Marco said you'd already made up."

Marco put his hands on his hips. "Well, Jules is sitting in his lap. Do you think he'd be doing that if they were still fighting?"

"Were you peeking in the window?" Bobby asked, already knowing the answer.

Marco had the decency to turn a nice shade of red. "They told me to."

"Liar," Kent grumbled.

Marco narrowed his eyes at Kent and Bobby knew that was his cue. "Well, on that note, we're outta here. Sorry about poker night, but some things are more important."

* * * *

Bobby cried Jules' name. He didn't know that his ass had ever been ridden as hard as Jules pounded into him. As much as the fucking broached that fine line between pleasure and pain, Bobby knew Jules would never intentionally hurt him. He'd been the one who'd asked Jules to give him everything he had, and boy, was Jules giving it to him.

"Want me to stop?" Jules panted.

"Hell, no." Bobby hitched his hips up further, giving Jules a new angle to plough into. Fuck, his body was on fire with the need to come, but he reached down and wrapped his hands around his sac. Not yet.

"Do you know how sexy you look?" Jules asked.

Yeah, Bobby was sure he looked real fucking sexy with his dark hair plastered to his face with sweat. He was sure he resembled some sort of freak contortionist from a circus sideshow, but goddamn, was it worth it.

"I'm gonna come," Jules warned.

"Yeah, yeah, do it," Bobby begged, biting the inside of his cheek.

Jules' cock plunged in once more and began to jerk as his lover climaxed, filling the condom no doubt.

Bobby released the hold he had on his balls and let his orgasm overtake him. He wasn't even sure how many times his cock shot its seed, but it was enough to leave him light-headed and shaking.

Jules gathered him in his arms and kissed him. "You okay?"

Bobby nodded, still floating on waves of pleasure. "I'm fantastic."

Jules chuckled and kissed him again. "I can't remember, ever feeling something so…"

"Yeah," Bobby agreed.

Jules fell to the side, and Bobby curled his body around his man. "I love you."

Jules grinned sleepily. "I love you, too."

On the drive over from Zac's, Bobby had plenty of time to think about what Jules had told him. He'd had an epiphany and needed to talk it over with his new partner. He swirled his finger around Jules' nipple. "Ya know, I think I bought *My Second Chance* to try and replace the empty place in my soul after losing *The Gypsy*."

"I can see that," Jules said, kissing Bobby's forehead.

"Well, I know it's been sixteen years, but you're not…" *Shit. How do I say this without coming off like an ass?*

Bobby took a deep breath and continued. "It's really me you want, right? I mean, I'm not just a replacement, am I?"

Jules rolled on top of Bobby and sat on his chest. "God no."

Jules leaned down until his face was an inch from Bobby's. "I loved Morgan, but I wasn't even the same man then. Hell, I don't even know if the two of us would still be together if he hadn't died. What I have with you, is me, finally living in the here and now, instead of the past. Does that make sense?"

Bobby nodded. "So what do you think I should do about my boat?"

"I think you should make it the best damn boat you can. You've already told me that *The Gypsy* no longer stirs the same feelings it once did, so walk away from it. Start your life over again with *My Second Chance*, let the boat live up to its name."

"How'd you get so damn smart?" Bobby asked, lifting his head to nip Jules' plump lower lip.

"I could say the school of hard knocks, but it was probably Yale," Jules chuckled.

Chapter Nine

"Hell, I fold." Kent tossed his cards on the table.

Bobby studied Zac. He knew his best friend better than anyone else present and although he'd never told him, Bobby could always tell when Zac was bluffing. Zac's tell wasn't in his face, it was in his feet. When Zac was riding on a shit hand, he tended to curl his feet up under his chair.

Bobby swept the floor in front of Zac with his feet. He picked up three ten-dollar chips and tossed them into the pile. Although he wanted his friend's money, he didn't want to totally screw the guy. "Call and raise you ten."

With the bet back in Zac's court, Bobby waited. Would his friend continue the charade or suck up his loss?

Zac tossed in thirty dollars. "What've you got?" he asked, laying down a pair of eights, Ace high.

Bobby grinned and flashed Zac his cards. "I got a couple of lovely ladies that need new dresses. Thanks for the money."

He scooped the pot towards him and began stacking his chips. "I appreciate it, boys. I should have enough after tonight's game to put the old girl into the water next weekend, and you're all invited."

Zac reached over and slapped Bobby on the back. "Congratulations, man."

"Can we bring a date?" Angelo asked, sipping some kind of crazy-assed drink he'd stirred up.

Marco slapped the table laughing.

Angelo looked completely perturbed. "What's so funny about that?"

"You, having a date's what's funny. When's the last time you went out?"

Bobby kicked Marco under the table. Although Angelo tried to act like Marco's ribbing wasn't bothering him, Bobby could tell by the way Angelo kept looking away that it did.

"Leave him alone, Marco." Bobby regarded Angelo. "Sure you can bring a date."

"When did you say it was?" Trey asked.

"Next Saturday," Bobby answered, shuffling the cards. He could swear Trey was blushing. It was a little hard to tell with Trey's light milk chocolate skin, but he could swear there was a red flush working its way up the man's face.

"I...um...don't think I'll be able to make it. I have a date," Trey confessed.

"So, bring him along. He can chat with Angelo's date," Marco laughed.

Bobby kicked Marco again.

"Ow. Dammit, stop doing that."

"Then keep your smartass comments to yourself."

"No. I don't think so," Trey replied uncomfortably. "It's a blind date."

"He's blind?" Marco asked, quickly putting his feet up on the table and out of Bobby's way.

Bobby reached over and pushed Marco out of his chair. The smaller man started laughing so hard he began to choke. Bobby rolled his eyes and shook his head. "Well, if you change your mind, we'll be at the marina in Pillar Point."

"Okay, thanks," Trey said.

Bobby dealt out the cards. "We'll go with Zac's favourite game, Texas Hold 'em. Although he sucks at it, Jules wants a new hammock on the deck of the new house, and I promised to bring home enough money to buy him one."

Jules had agreed to put his sister's house up for sale a month earlier. They'd figured it would take a while to sell, but lo and behold, it had taken only four days. When Jules asked Bobby where he'd like to start their new life together, Bobby had jumped on the area south of the city.

They ended up finding the perfect place just south of Pacifica. It was on the water and had an awesome deck and that was the only thing either of them cared about. As he played the first hand, he kept glancing at the clock.

"What the hell is going on?" Kent asked.

"Huh?"

"You just totally flashed your cards at me."

"Did not," Bobby refuted.

"Really? So you don't have two sevens and a ten?"

"Fuck." Bobby threw his cards on the table. "Would you guys be pissed if I took off?"

"The Doc home tonight?" Zac asked.

"Yeah. He was supposed to put in his two-week notice."

Zac lowered his cards. "He's quitting?"

Bobby nodded. It had been totally Jules' idea, but Bobby had supported his lover all the way. "He's going to work part-time at the hospital in Daly City. It'll be a lot closer to home and fewer hours of course."

Zac whistled. "I wonder how Eric's gonna take it. You know Jules is, like, his hero."

Bobby grinned. He knew, and so did Jules. "Jules said after Eric gets a few more years in the trenches under his belt, he'd help him get a job anywhere he wanted."

"Seriously? That would be cool."

Bobby handed his chips to Angelo. "Cash me out, Ang. I've got a man to go see."

* * * *

"Now this is my idea of the proper way to christen a yacht," Bobby groaned, reaching for the lube. The party had been a success, but Bobby was glad when it was time for his friends to go home. He'd led his lover down to the captain's cabin with the intention of ravishing him on the open waters. Yeah, he was pirate captain Bobby and Jules was his cabin boy.

"It was a nice party, but what was with Angelo and his date?" Jules asked, spreading his legs.

Bobby slicked his fingers and reached down to run them across Jules' puckered hole. "Why are we talking about Angelo and his boring date?"

"Because lately we can't go an hour without fucking. So, if I want to talk to you it has to be done during."

"Oh, okay, makes sense."

"So? Who was the stiff with Angelo?" Jules asked around a moan.

"I don't remember his name. I think he's a banker of some kind. The thing about Angelo is he thinks he needs some rich, fancy intellectual guy. I'm not sure if that's his doing or his mother's." Angelo's mother was truly a piece of work. To call Ang a momma's boy was an understatement.

Removing his fingers, Bobby positioned himself between Jules' legs. "Enough talking."

He pressed his cock against Jules' stretched hole and slowly sunk in to the hilt. Zing! Just like always, a bolt of sexual electricity travelled up his spine to the back of his neck. It didn't seem to matter how many times he'd made love to Jules, it was exciting every time.

"Do you want it hard and fast, or slow and easy?"

Jules bit his lip. "How about slow and hard, turning into fast and easy?"

Bobby grinned. "Leave it to you to think outside the box."

Pulling out slowly, Bobby thrust back in hard, jarring both bodies. After several plunges, Jules' head came to rest against the wall.

"Hmmm, next time I'll have to tie your feet to the bottom of the bed," Bobby teased, repositioning them lower on the mattress.

Jules leaned up and gave Bobby a deep kiss. "Let me turn over."

Bobby pulled out and waited for his lover to get on his knees with his ass high in the air. Kneeling behind Jules, Bobby plunged back inside. It said a lot about their relationship that this was now one of Jules' favourite positions. No longer did he need to see Bobby's face to know who was making love to him.

As his rhythm began to pick up, his cell phone rang. Bobby ignored it in favour of changing angles slightly. The new position had Jules going wild.

"Oh, yeah, there, oh, shit." Jules groaned, thrusting back on Bobby's cock.

Bobby reached down and wrapped a hand around Jules' erection, pressing his thumb into the oozing slit. His cell phone rang again, as he bit the soft area between Jules' shoulder blades.

"Come on, babe, come on, give it to your captain," Bobby grunted.

Jules yelled his climax loud enough the seagulls on deck took flight in a squawk of irritation.

Bobby continued to piston his hips, burying his cock hard and fast in the man he loved. Jules was the first and last man to ever get his naked cock inside him and Bobby couldn't believe what a difference it made.

Hell, just the thought of filling his lover's ass with his cum tipped Bobby over the edge. He ground his groin against Jules' ass as he let loose a torrent of seed. Jules' cell phone rang as Bobby pushed him to the mattress and lay on top of him.

"Someone wants to talk to you in a big way," Jules mumbled into the pillow.

"Probably just Brad, trying once again to get me to buy *The Gypsy*." Bobby had washed his hands of his family and his old boat, and felt like a new man for doing it.

Jules rose up and rolled Bobby off him. "Unfortunately, I'm a doctor, and can't ignore a ringing phone."

Bobby lay on his back, sucking much needed oxygen into his lungs as Jules reached for his phone.

"Hello?"

"Uh, yeah, hold on." Jules held the phone out to Bobby. "It's Zac. He doesn't sound good."

Bobby's heart thudded against his chest as he took the phone. "Hey, Zac."

"Trey's been hurt. He's at San Francisco General. Eric and I are on the way."

"Trey? What happened?" Bobby felt Jules stiffen beside him and pulled his lover against his chest.

"I don't know. The hospital said he had me down as an emergency contact and that he'd need me when he came out of surgery."

"But they don't know what happened?"

"The police responded to a domestic disturbance at Trey's house. They found him beaten…"

Zac paused and Bobby could tell there was something else.

"And?" he asked.

"There were signs of rape."

Bobby closed his eyes. Trey was one of the gentlest men he knew. What kind of animal took advantage of someone like that? "We'll get there as soon as possible. Don't forget to tell the police he had a blind date."

"Already taken care of. Eric's on the phone with Kent right now. We'll meet you up there."

Bobby hung up and turned to Jules. "We need to get to San Francisco General. Trey's been raped and beaten."

"My God," Jules gasped, springing off the bed.

After a quick clean-up, they were dressed and on the road. Bobby sat in the passenger seat relaying to Jules everything Zac had told him.

"Should we call his family?" Jules asked.

Bobby shook his head. "They haven't spoken to Trey in a while. I think that should be his call."

Jules reached over and took Bobby's hand. "We'll get him through this. We can move him in with us if we need to."

Bobby squeezed his love's hand. "Thanks. I know you didn't plan on all this when we decided to move in together."

Jules shook his head. "Not so. I knew the moment I saw you with your friends that you all were a package deal. Fortunately for me, I happen to adore your friends."

"I'm glad, because they mean everything to me."

"As they should," Jules agreed.

About the Author

An avid reader for years, one day Carol Lynne decided to write her own brand of erotic romance. Carol juggles between being a full-time mother and a full-time writer. These days, you can usually find Carol either cleaning jelly out of the carpet or nestled in her favourite chair writing steamy love scenes.

Carol loves to hear from readers. You can find her contact information, website details and author profile page at http://www.total-e-bound.com

Total-E-Bound Publishing

www.total-e-bound.com

Take a look at our exciting range of literagasmic™
erotic romance titles and discover pure quality
at Total-E-Bound.

www.ingramcontent.com/pod-product-compliance
Lightning Source LLC
Chambersburg PA
CBHW032030240626
47154CB00003B/856